What people are say

Travelers

Donald Altman's *Travelers* is a gripping mystical journey through Time and Space, rooted in the reality of a Psychiatric Hospital. A Psychiatrist journeys into his young patient's universe and together they fight his inner demons which turn out to be both real and imagined. The outer demons make this book a real thriller in the unique microcosm of the Hospital which reverberates and expands to illuminate the forces unleashed in our world today. Both chilling and moving.
Lyle Kessler, Tony-Award nominated playwright and screenwriter of *Orphans* and *The Saint of Fort Washington*

The mutual reciprocity between Professional Care Giver and Under Cared For unfolds in various surprising and meaningful ways in this fascinating novel, and reminds me of *K-Pax*; of Ken Kesey's hero's Herculean labors to free the prisoners of Nurse Ratchet and her over-institutionalized mental health system; as well as initiatory and cosmic healing journeys of all kinds, outer and inner and beyond, physical, mental, spiritual, emotional— during which the shadows in the fearsome heart of darkness are revealed as nothing less than the light of spiritual love itself. It is insights like Dr. Banks' profound pith instruction, "Just remember no one is either all bad or all good," that makes *Travelers* worth reading and savoring in the heart of awakened awareness during these tumultuous, confused and stressful times.
Lama Surya Das, author of *Awakening the Buddha Within*

Donald Altman's *Travelers* is a brilliant and beautiful journey into the mystical realms of mind, body, and spirit healing. It

is so well written that it immediately draws you into the story of a psychiatrist's spiritual initiation. It is written from the perspective of someone who has spent countless hours working with patients, studying mindfulness and exploring the vast realms of the interiority. *Travelers* is an odyssey of hope, healing and the holistic integration of our fragmented selves.
Michael Stone, trauma facilitator and author of *Living a Shamanic Way of Life*

Travelers is a powerful and touching novel of loss, grief and healing. In the tradition of Herman Hesse, this thought-provoking story carries you into new realms of the psyche as it follows the main character in his search for authenticity, self-knowledge, and spirituality. Its timeless message is how love is given, not taken.
John Arden, PhD, psychologist and author of *Mind-Brain-Gene*

Travelers is a thrilling adventure and journey into the uncharted world of shamanic visions, paranormal states and new dimensions of consciousness. A clinical psychiatrist's theories, personal life, and medical career are jeopardized through his chance encounter with a mysterious "traveler" at the psych hospital. Donald Altman draws on his extensive experiences as a psychotherapist, former monk and spiritual seeker to weave a narrative full of twists and turns, as compelling as it is inspiring.
David Nez, author of *Tree of Visions: Visionary Traditions of the Western World*

Travelers promises a spiritual journey of significance and Altman's book delivers. While it reads like a true story written by a therapist, the story carries you along on a mystical journey of initiation into another reality. This novel challenges what you assume to be true and how your beliefs can limit you. The story reveals the deeper truth of how those who unexpectedly

show up in your life can open your heart and help you consider possibilities beyond the known. The grieving protagonist experiences a deep transformation, and the reader is invited to a deeper understanding of self as well.
Julie Tallard Johnson, LCSW, author of *The Clue of the Red Thread* and *Wheel of Initiation*

Travelers is a marvelous book that shows how we all have our little mental boxes, and for psychiatrist Dr. Ben Banks, his have become a prison cell. Then, a new patient, young Mason Delabrey, with his mind-blowing experiences, comes for help. And the boy's therapy quickly becomes a two-way street that broadens the doctor's limited perception of himself and his possibilities—even those that exist after death. Something we all need. Highly recommended.
John Nelson, visionary author of *I, Human* and *Matrix of the Gods*

Read this book to open your doors of perception! This story casts a quantum spell, triggering "spooky action at a distance" within you. Like the works of Carlos Castaneda, *Travelers* takes you on a journey beyond the limits of rationality and science that will have you questioning reality. *Travelers* is sure to leave an enduring echo of hope reverberating in your heart and spirit long after the words recede into memory. A deeply soul satisfying and meaningful work for our times.
Randall Fitzgerald, author and former Roving Editor of *Reader's Digest*

Travelers is a beautifully crafted story of the journey of Dr. Banks, a trained psychiatrist coping with his own inner pains and demons along with those of his patients. The author's professional knowledge of the inner workings of a psychiatric hospital create such vivid reality that the reader wonders if the story is biography, fiction or science fiction. The reader is drawn effortlessly into the town and hospital and home of Dr. Banks, and accepts the strange and wondrous visitors and visions that come to ease his personal pain. The very human struggle for finding truth and healing adds a veracity to a well-drawn and compelling story that allows the reader to ponder their own attitudes toward the spiritual unknown with greater insight. *Travelers* is a quick read but contains depths of knowledge that teach and enlighten and ends with a positive appreciation of the individual potential that exists inside us all. Highly recommended.

Doug Lowell, author of *Soulmate*

Travelers

Travelers

Donald Altman

ROUNDFIRE
BOOKS

Winchester, UK
Washington, USA

JOHN HUNT PUBLISHING

First published by Roundfire Books, 2023
Roundfire Books is an imprint of John Hunt Publishing Ltd., No. 3 East St., Alresford,
Hampshire SO24 9EE, UK
office@jhpbooks.com
www.johnhuntpublishing.com
www.roundfire-books.com

For distributor details and how to order please visit the 'Ordering' section on our website.

Text copyright: Donald Altman 2021

ISBN: 978 1 80341 094 4
978 1 80341 095 1 (ebook)
Library of Congress Control Number: 2021949918

A CIP catalogue record for this book is available from the British Library.

Design: Stuart Davies

UK: Printed and bound by CPI Group (UK) Ltd, Croydon, CR0 4YY
Printed in North America by CPI GPS partners

We operate a distinctive and ethical publishing philosophy in
all areas of our business, from our global network of authors to
production and worldwide distribution.

Books by Donald Altman

The Power of Pause
Simply Mindful: A 7-Week Guide and Personal Handbook for Mindful Living
The Mindfulness Toolbox
101 Mindful Ways to Build Resilience
One Minute Mindfulness
Reflect: Awaken to the Wisdom of the Here and Now
Clearing Emotional Clutter
The Mindfulness Code
Simply Mindful Coloring Book
Living Kindness
The Mindfulness Toolbox for Relationships
Art of the Inner Meal
Meal by Meal
Eat, Savor, Satisfy: 12-Weeks to Mindful Eating
The Joy Compass

Acknowledgments

To my *Bak'u del cuore* Maria, my soul friend and life partner—
thank you for infusing these pages with a wealth of insightful
and joyful creative ideas, as well as your uplifting spirit. I am
indebted to my family, especially my mother, Barbara, who
continues to be a shining light and spiritual guide.

I will always be thankful for the compassionate teachings
of the Venerable U. Silananda and my spiritual brother U.
Thitzana.

My thanks for the helpful and generous offering of ideas
from Gabe Lee, John Nelson, Randy Fitzgerald, John Babbitt,
John Arden, Linda Struble and others. I am grateful to John
Hunt Publishing and the staff of G.L. Davies, Dominic James,
Charlotte Anne Edwards, Denise Smith, Nick Welch, Krystina
Kellingley and others, for your creativity, enthusiasm and
collaborative spirit.

My deep gratitude extends to teachers, students, persons
and spiritual friends who made this book possible. Finally, my
thanks go to you, dear readers and Travelers, who will complete
the circle of this offering and bring to life the ideas contained in
these pages.

Blessings all!

To My Fellow Stardust Travelers—
May we help those travelers we encounter each day,
in ways both large and small.

And, as an ancient blessing advises:
May suffering ones be suffering free,
May the fear struck fearless be,
May grieving ones shed all grief,
May all beings find relief.

And as we awaken,
May we all travel in peace.

Chapter 1

Let me start this book with an apology of sorts. You see, I am a board-certified psychiatrist, not a book writer. I've written an occasional article here and there, but I'm most comfortable making diagnostic assessments, writing chart notes and documenting sessions with patients at a large hospital's psychiatric unit in Oregon where I have worked for over fifteen years. To remove any confusion, let me disclose upfront that I have no affiliation with the Oregon State Hospital. That's where they filmed *One Flew Over the Cuckoo's Nest* and have a nearby museum where you can still see Big Indian's broom and the hydrotherapy room. That story, I assure you, was pure fiction. What I'm about to share with you, on the other hand, is an accurate rendition of events to the best of my ability. Naturally, for reasons of confidentiality, I have changed all the names, as well as any details that might reveal the actual persons involved. Still, the key events themselves are undeniable.

One more thing needs to be clearly stated before I launch into this case. You may not think that psychiatrists are scientists, but we undergo intense medical training, learn best practices, and use a combination of neuroleptics and other meds with proven talk therapy approaches to help patients. I only mention that because what I'm about to share in these pages may seem to be "out there," in the sense that it lacks rationality and science-based evidence.

For that reason, I have drawn extensively from my notes, as well as recollections from my journal to assemble them into a single, cohesive story. If there is any fault in the telling of events, that is my own, and my own completely. Again, not being a writer, I hope you'll permit me the benefit of adding the word "cohesive" — if I may be so optimistic as to do so.

This case precipitated with the arrival of a young man, Mason Delabrey, age 19, at the hospital for evaluation. When he first arrived in my office, Mason looked so thin that I wondered if he was emaciated. He was dressed all in black, and his straight, long black hair hung low over his forehead making it difficult to see his eyes. When I held out my hand to shake his, Mason retreated inwardly. Uncertain yet hopeful, I kept my arm outstretched. It was only after an awkward pause that he hesitantly reached out to greet me. Though his hand was quite cold, I noticed his nails were not brittle. Neither could I see any lanugo hair on his face or neck—the furry or fine hair that is sometimes present with anorexia and which serves as the body's strategy for preserving heat. Still, I made a mental note to check for disordered eating. However, the most salient issue on his admission report which I'd be addressing in my initial intake was an attempted suicide.

Mason chose to sit on the red sofa in my office. Seeing this, I joined him in a nearby, adjacent chair, so as not to sit behind a desk. I tried to match his posture, even subtly. He watched me through his long bangs, which he swept aside for a moment. There, I finally saw his entire face; it was soft and as white as a pearl with an anathema to the sun. His nose was long and slender, and his eyebrows, set beneath a large forehead, furrowed over his large brown eyes, all lending to an expression that seemed perpetually questioning and melancholy.

"You body matching me?" he asked. There was not the slightest hint of hostility in his tone, only a sense of curiosity.

"Body matching?" I asked.

"Mocking my movements."

Caught off guard, I paused. I had gotten in the habit of doing this to attune to patients, but I couldn't remember the last time a patient pointed this out. In rapid succession, a few possible responses to Mason's query ran through my head. Finally, I realized if I was to connect with this young man, I needed to fess up.

"I'm not going to B.S. you, Mason. You're right. But, I didn't do it in a deceitful way. Sometimes it helps me sense what others are feeling. You're very observant," I said, purposely pointing out one of his strengths—and wondering how he would respond.

"So tell me, what am I feeling?" he insisted, not letting me off the hook.

I pressed my hands together and raised them up until my forefingers touched my lips. Taking a breath, my chest heaved slightly on the exhale.

"I don't know." I shook my head. "I was hoping you'd tell me." Instead of sharing, he just stared down at the floor. So, I thought I'd break the ice by explaining that I didn't like to do standard tests, such as giving patients the Beck Depression Inventory or any of the anxiety inventories during an initial intake. I simply wanted to enter a person's world and see how I might gain understanding before coming to any conclusions, diagnostic or otherwise. "I do know that you're in pain. Life is a continuum of experiences, and the best I can tell you, Mason, is that I've learned not to judge. So, I hope you'll share with me..."

"What? Why I tried to kill myself?" he interrupted.

"Yes, I do want to know that. But what I was going to say was, 'I hope you'll share whatever can help me to help you.'"

There was another long period of silence. As I sat, I noticed a shaft of light coming through the screened window and forming a rectangle on the worn beige carpet between Mason's feet and my own. I was just about to break in when he shared a rather vivid hallucination experience, as follows from sections of my chart notes and memory:

The patient's affect was somewhat flat as he began talking:

"I don't ever remember anything being so completely black. So black so that it made me catch my breath. I jerked my head from side to side to see where I was, but there was just this empty darkness. I remember clenching my hands and I could feel the coldness of my fingers in my palms. It felt good to feel them."

The patient reported peering into the darkness when an arm reached forward, as if out of a cloud of nothingness. When I asked if this startled him, Mason stated he "wasn't afraid," which struck him as kind of "weirdly different." He reported being more curious than anything. It was in this state of openness that he simply watched as the arm, an apparently disembodied arm, reached upwards and towards the side of his head.

The fingers, long and thin, touched him ever so gently on his left temple. With that, a hoarse, almost whispering voice asked him, "Are you a traveler?"

Upon hearing this question, the patient reported thinking, "Am I a traveler? What does that mean?" The patient pondered over this question as the fingers continued to lightly touch his temple. They felt warm to the touch, somehow inviting. Even though the body from which the arm reached out was not visible, this entity, or whatever it was, made him feel safe. Although he wasn't a hundred percent sure, something inside told him what to say: "Yes. Yes, I'm a traveler."

What happened next was abbreviated in my notes, but I'd like to share it here in its entirety. Mason said that someone, or *something*, dressed in a black shawl stepped out from the veil of darkness. When I asked Mason about any identifying features, he reported that because the figure was hooded, he was unable to describe any details about the face or even the sex.

Then, unexpectedly, in the blink of an eye this figure bear-hugged him. At that moment, according to the patient, "the blackness was suddenly replaced with the brightness of white light, white all over, a white so bright that for a moment it blinded me." Simultaneously, he felt himself being catapulted upward, like a cannonball.

With this sense of upward movement came an overwhelming feeling he had never known before. It was, he described, like being enveloped in "a warm glow, kind of sweet, like warm honey and roses." The glow, along with the sweet fragrance and sense of lightness, was intoxicating. It occurred to him for a moment that maybe this was like meeting God, but as soon as that thought occurred, the whiteness and light cleared away.

Suddenly, Mason realized he was in a garage, floating up near the ceiling. Before any thoughts could interfere, he recognized various objects like a rusty rake with a broken handle, the bent garbage can, the blue mountain bike. The word "Damn!" popped into his head with the realization that this wasn't just any garage, but the garage at his parent's home. He lived here!

Mason noticed that the garage was smoky, and the car was running. He felt his body descending, attracted to the car like a magnet, even though he hadn't consciously told it where to move. That's when he saw a figure collapsed across the front seat.

According to Mason, his body again moved without effort. He felt himself contacting and moving through the car door, which was still shut. He hovered closer to the body. He was looking at a profile of a pale face; the eyes were half shut, and each breath was heavy and labored. Suddenly it dawned on him. This young man was himself.

In my office, Mason screamed aloud, "Noooo!" as if he were reliving the moment. Although I am trained to be professionally neutral, I felt a chill surge through my body. I asked the patient to take a few slow breaths before telling me what he saw. After feeling composed again, he described a crushing pain.

No longer was he floating and witnessing. Instead, it was like a thousand needles pierced him. He tried to move his body, but each limb was heavy like large rocks. It took every ounce of his remaining strength to press the "off" button on the car's dash. His arm slid over to the horn, which he pressed and pressed repeatedly while gasping and choking for air. The last thing he remembered thinking, he told me, was, "Please take my head out of this fucking vice."

Mason's next memory was waking up in the hospital with an IV drip in his arm. Before our session was up, we talked at length about what this traveler experience meant to him. Had he ever heard this traveler "voice" before? It was well recognized in the field that the first symptoms of schizophrenia often developed in late adolescence with hallucinations and delusions. But Mason's experience seemed unusual to me, and I'd have to rule out other possible physical causes, including a brain concussion history.

Before our time was up, I asked Mason about his suicide and said that I wanted him to be safe. I was relieved when he promised not to harm himself and that he was willing to work on a safety plan with me. As he stood to leave my office, he paused at the door.

"Can you call my mom?" His voice was quivering, trailing off. "Tell her I'm sorry…"

"Sorry for what?"

"For this, for everything, for being such a fuck-up." He stood frozen, looking blankly at the floor.

I cupped my hand ever so gently on the back of his shoulder, which felt so frail that I could clearly feel his scapula. "I'll be talking to her. Would you like me to arrange for you to see her?"

A small, fragile voice, somewhere from deep inside of this

six-foot tall young man answered with a single word, "Okay," before shuffling out the door where an orderly was waiting to show him to his room.

Composing my SOAP notes (that's psycho-lingo for one way to format and structure notes on a session: the Subjective, the Objective, the Assessment, and the Plan), I realized that even if his suicide attempt was caused by a triggering event, Mason clearly suffered from anhedonia and other signs of acute depression. The only thing he reportedly got pleasure from was drawing and sketching, but he had stopped doing those activities months ago.

Under the Plan section of my notes, I wrote that Mason might benefit from being included in a group with our excellent art therapist, David. There was certainly enough reason to keep him hospitalized until we eliminated any possible self-harm and had his diagnosis and meds sorted out.

Most patients on my residential unit were a fair bit older than Mason. They were severely impaired, delusional and in crisis. Typically, they remained here for two or three weeks until they were stabilized on meds and returned to their home or family. Unfortunately, the families didn't always welcome them back, and so more than a few ended up on the streets, biding their time until they boomeranged back to us. Mason didn't really seem to fit in with our milieu, but we'd just have to make it work.

"Hey, it's Bono! Oh my God, I love U2, you are so awesome!" A manic patient, Roy, beamed at me as I headed down the hall to a staff meeting.

"Hi, Roy," I smiled.

"You gonna play something for us? I can't believe Bono is here. Look!" he said to Mr. Dibby, a middle-aged man with unipolar depression who rarely spoke. Mr. Dibby looked up, obviously unimpressed by my Bono impression.

"Coffee!!!" came a shout from Wanda, a thin older woman

who was seated in the common area and could never seem to get enough caffeine.

"Is your rib open?" asked Frita, a slender woman in her thirties.

"No, I think it's my jacket."

"Coffee!!!" called out Wanda again, to no one in particular.

"Bono, don't go! No, not before you sing," pleaded Roy from behind.

"I'm not going anywhere, Roy. I'll check in on you later, okay?"

"'Sunday Bloody Sunday', man!" My biggest fan moved and gyrated wildly.

"That's wrong," demanded Burt, a fifty-year-old who was diagnosed with schizoaffective disorder. "You don't know what you're doing. I work here and you can't do that!" Burt grabbed another patient's coffee and spilled it all over himself. "I'm wet! I'm wet! Oh my God, I'm wet!" he shouted, trying to wipe the coffee off his shirt and pants.

"How do you get a cup of coffee around here? I paid for it! Coffee!!!" echoed in the hall behind me as I walked past the nurses' station and turned down the hall.

Yes, these patients were sometimes delusional and might act out, but they weren't scary violent like those living in the forensic unit of our hospital. I had spent time working on the forensic side, and it was no fun always looking over your shoulder to make sure you weren't getting assaulted.

The most frightening patient in forensics was the behemoth of a man nicknamed "Sasquatch." This name was not chosen lightly. Sasquatch stood almost seven feet tall. He refused to cut his hair or shave his beard, both of which were hopelessly matted and accentuated the impression of his being a dangerous, fierce and wooly animal. He lumbered about the unit clumsily, each foot slapping at the ground as his arms swung wildly along for the ride. He was probably over-medicated on Haldol, which might have accounted for the atypical body movement, but no doctor wanted to be responsible for reducing the dose of his antipsychotic cocktail.

He was in his mid-twenties, after an already long history of assault, paranoia and delusions, that Sasquatch tragically stabbed his brother in the eye and his sister in the throat with a carving knife at the family Thanksgiving dinner table. The sister bled out and died before the EMTs arrived, and the brother lost an eye. Sasquatch seemed genuinely remorseful about what he had done. While he rarely heard voices anymore like the one that told him to attack his brother and sister, he never pleaded for his release when his time came up for a mandatory court appearance. His mother continued to visit him with site supervision, but his father and brother refused to acknowledge him. Unlike those forensic patients who made progress and left the unit for weekend visits with family, Sasquatch was most likely a lifer.

I found a seat and settled in for the staff meeting around the rectangular table along with my unit's other two clinicians, psychiatrist Dr. Rick Milton and Licensed Professional Counselor Sarah Brown. Also in attendance was our art therapist, David, and our pharmacist, Mitch. Sitting at the head of the table and leading the group was Executive Director of the hospital, Dr. Beverly Howell. She oversaw the operation of all the units and had been here since the hospital's inception twenty-five years prior. Beverly's rosy complexion made her seem warm and approachable. But make no mistake. When her piercing brown eyes, framed by gray hair flecked with black undertones, turned in your direction, she communicated a very different impression. With Beverly you always knew where you stood, and she was usually right.

When my turn came to present the status of my cases, I started with Mason. In particular, I raised a concern as to whether he needed our level of hospital care. Wouldn't a depression treatment center for young adults be a better fit? In response, Beverly divulged that the boy's parents had requested and received, a mental health commitment hold. This had been pending, but was just approved by the court. She slid a thick packet of papers across the table in my direction.

"His father, Edward Delabrey, is a very influential attorney who has assisted this hospital on numerous occasions. So I want to be sure we offer him, uh, and his family, every accommodation."

It flashed in my mind who she was talking about. Five years earlier, the hospital was sued for not protecting patients from a male nurse who had a history of sexually abusing patients in another state. He moved to Oregon, but the hospital didn't do a thorough background check. Edward Delabrey had successfully represented the hospital in a high profile court case in which he discredited the female patient who had accused the nurse. He saved the hospital millions, but the whole incident left a bad taste in my mouth. Apparently, Delabrey's law firm was on retainer and continued to help the hospital with all kinds of legal issues.

"The utilization manager says we've been low on census," continued Beverly. "That's not a reason to keep him, obviously, but that report gives us more than enough reason to admit him, possibly long term."

Glancing at the court order, I couldn't disagree. I saw the list of reasons why Mason's mother and father had co-signed the mental health hold. The evidence showed that Mason had been refusing depression medication prescribed by his family doctor, had threatened self-harm, and was recently caught lighting fireworks and setting off the fire alarm at his father's law office. There was also the mention of an assault against a family member, but no details of that assault were given nor was any official charge ever made. Mason hadn't shared this information with me, and the assault was something I'd have to clarify in our next session.

I must admit, I had to stifle a smile when reading about the fire alarm episode. There were times, I thought, when I would have wanted to do something like that to rattle my own father's sense of propriety and smugness. Strangely, this stirred a memory about mythic philosopher and storyteller Michael Meade and his work on the father-son dynamic. I made a mental note to consider bringing Meade's concepts into my work with this young man. While Mason's outbreak at his father's office hardly seemed reason enough for commitment, he certainly exhibited a pattern of behavior that was concerning. Just as I concluded the case discussion, David piped up and suggested that Mason might be a good fit for his art therapy group. I agreed and said I'd schedule him for it.

By the end of the day, as I wrapped up loose ends and filed away my notes, I felt a weariness overcome me. My mind was spinning with all that I'd have to unpack in my next meeting with Mason. That would include making a decision on meds and a definitive diagnosis, such as schizophrenia, unless I could rule that out. I'd also need to arrange to meet with his family and get greater insight into Mason's behavior and the family dynamics—and learn about the assaults.

I looked out my window to check the weather. It was still dry out, despite a mix of clouds and sun. The heart-shaped leaves on the white-trunked aspen trees had already fallen, which was not surprising given it was late October. I put on my hat and jacket, and entered in my code to unlock the only door to the unit.

"Goodnight, Dr. Banks," said our perpetually sanguine, red-headed receptionist by the main entrance.

"Goodnight, Fran," I said, forcing a smile.

Outside, the chilly air stung my face. I noticed the topiary shrubs alongside the walkway looked a little ragged, and I wondered how our longtime gardener Reggie could have possibly missed this.

The sky was streaked with long strands of pink and yellow. "Damn, another summer on the way out," I mused wistfully, "I wonder how many more of these I'll see?" I hinged open the creaky, metal gate leading to the street. Each time I opened that gate, it reminded me of my own creaky knees that had caused me to abandon jogging.

A few steps away, near my car, I spotted a short woman with long and bushy dark brown hair moving slowly along the sidewalk. She wore faded jeans and an unusual, multi-colored jacket. A large backpack hung from her stout frame and thick shoulders. I thought I saw something move, and I was surprised to see a small black and white spaniel balancing on her shoulders. As she knelt down to remove the backpack, the spaniel leapt down from its hairy perch.

After putting my briefcase inside the trunk of my car, the dog pranced up to me, tail wagging.

"Hey, nice dog." I bent down to pet the pooch's head.

"His name is Bear." The dog's owner smiled at me. Her face was round, her hair framing warm and inquisitive green eyes. Her skin was deeply tanned and leathery from exposure to the elements. "Damn, another summer on the way out. Makes you wonder just how many more of these you'll see, don't it?" As she finished, she gave me a sly wink.

Her exact repetition of what I had thought just moments earlier stopped me in my tracks. "Uh, yeah. I was just thinking that."

"Gonna be getting cold soon. Bear and me be hitting the road, headed south to warm weather."

"So you don't live around here?" My eyes were drawn to a tassel hanging from her hair. Woven into the tassel was a long white feather. It caressed the side of her head and glistened like a jewel in the fading sunlight.

"Oh no," she guffawed. The feather floated up and down, as

if in agreement. "Nah, just stayed for the summer. We don't live nowhere. Me and Bear, we's travelers."

"Travelers?" I spit out reflexively. It seemed a strange coincidence so soon after hearing Mason's hallucination, but as I recalled from my time poring over Jung's *Red Book*, there are no coincidences, only the manifestation of parallel events that live beyond the fringes of chance and probability.

"Yeah, I ain't no panhandler. I don't ask for money." She started digging into her backpack, stood up and held out a small, intricately woven metal wrapped pendant no larger than a thumbnail. "Here, look. I make these. This one here's a necklace. You can put a stone in here if you want."

"That's very nice," I nodded, inspecting the detailed handiwork.

"Takes me about 12 hours to make this. And I make these jackets, too." She extended her arms to model the creation, which was a patchwork of shapes and materials. She told me that the cuffs, which consisted of fabric adorned with metal holes, were recycled from old gym shoes.

"You're really creative." I pulled out my wallet and held out a $10 bill. "Please take this for you and Bear. Maybe you could use it?"

"Sure could, thanks," she grinned, displaying a couple of missing teeth.

She suddenly crouched down and began digging in her backpack. I looked on, curiously, and so did Bear. No more than five seconds passed when she bolted upright and presented me with a pristine business card. I couldn't believe that *anything* could come out of her crammed backpack without so much as a crease, a wrinkle or a smudge.

"Call me if you need anything. A necklace, or, well, I'm sure you need something I can offer, Ben." She winked mischievously at me.

I blinked in surprise. Had I told her my name? I didn't think so, and I felt a strong and immediate sense of unease. Besides, I had absolutely no idea what she was hinting at with her vague offer.

"Gotta find the trainyard. It's a big yard, called Albina. The Albina Train Yard. You know it?"

"Train. You mean riding the rails? Isn't that dangerous?"

"Ain't so bad. Only dangerous if the bulls get ya'. So long as you hop on or off outside of the yard, it's okay."

"The 'bulls'?"

"That's train security." She zipped shut the pack and lifted Bear back onto her neck. "You know where Albina is?"

"North Portland, I think."

"Oh, I'm Jacki," she said, holding out her hand. She had a firm grip as she pumped my arm up and down several times.

"Did I meet you or... How'd you know my name?"

"Oh. You told me, right? Or, sometimes I just knows things, ain't that right, Bear?" She chuckled and her dog barked, seemingly nodding its head. "I'm a traveler, so call me Traveler Jacki."

"In that case, Bear and, uhm, Traveler Jacki... Good luck."

"See ya' round, Ben."

For a few seconds I stood immobile, and everything seemed unnaturally quiet as I watched her walk along the sidewalk with Bear hunched low for the ride. I glanced at her card and found it contained no phone number. All it said was, *Traveler Jacki and Bear at Your Service. Jobs Big and Small.*

Oddly, when I got in my car and pulled forward, this unusual woman and her dog had seemingly vanished into thin air. Meeting her was discomforting, and I could only shrug my shoulders as I stuffed her bizarre calling card in my pocket.

Chapter 2

When I pulled into my driveway that evening, the lights were on inside the house. I knew what to expect before entering through the door from the garage. Beth would be curled up on one corner of the worn, purple upholstered sofa. A thick flowered pillow would prop her up, and a big box of knitting supplies, yarn and needles would sprawl beside her like a spider's web. This was a web that you would not go near. And when I say "you," what I really mean is that it's a web that "I" was not meant to go near.

Stepping inside, I heard Judge Judy's voice blaring from the TV like it did almost every night, harping on someone, telling them how stupid, selfish and irresponsible they were and how they needed to get a job, as if that was the answer to all of life's problems. In the living room I set down my briefcase on the far end of the sofa where I used to sit. No, I didn't need to put my briefcase here, but it helped me feel nearer to Beth, as strange as that may sound.

Beth looked so small, sitting there with a mound of yarn on her lap and legs crossed under her, like a knitting Buddha. Every now and then, as Judge Judy raised her voice to verbally berate someone, Beth would glance up without moving her head. Her maroon-framed glasses didn't move in the slightest as she looked back down at her knitting. Judge Judy, you see, was just another web separating us, one that I had learned not to breach.

"Hi, Beth." I always said this. It was my way of stepping ever so gently onto the web.

"Benjamin."

Her ignoring the implied "Hi" stung, but I'd gotten used to it. I tried my damn best to keep things normal, even though they weren't. I don't recall exactly when we stopped interacting at the end of the day. For much of our twenty years plus of marriage, we'd always enjoyed sharing a bold, berry-flavored glass of Cabernet Sauvignon in the evening, sometimes paired with aged Parmigiano-Reggiano, our favorite hard cheese. Living not too far from Oregon's wine country of the Willamette Valley, we preferred to go local whenever possible.

Sometimes I would bake fish, usually salmon or cod, and Beth would fix us a huge salad brimming with Swiss chard, broccoli, radish, tomatoes and carrots, all fresh from our garden. If cucumbers were available, she'd peel the outer skin and then run the fork tines lengthwise down the cucumber before slicing. I always joked that if anyone could transform a humble cucumber into royalty, it was Beth. I never ceased to marvel at how everything she did was accomplished with grace and aplomb.

During the summers, we'd set up on the patio in our small, secluded backyard. Blue-hooded stellar jays, crows and green hummingbirds often darted about for a drink from our fountain or seed from the bird feeder. If it was early spring, we'd be visited by the two-toned brown and white killdeer. Our daughter, Melissa, joined us most nights when not out with friends. Beth, who worked in HR for a large supplier of mechanical parts for the auto and marine industries, always had an amusing story to share with us about managing all the different personalities in a manufacturing plant.

But I think it was Melissa's glow, vibrancy and positive attitude that really made our meals fun and memorable. I'll always remember how thrilled Melissa was when the brightly adorned yellow and black American Goldfinch honored us with a rare visit. We called it "Mel's bird." She had created several pastel sketches and water color paintings of the finch, which we proudly displayed in her room and throughout the house.

Today, however, there was no garden for fresh salad, no delicious hard cheese to be paired with anything. There were no life experiences to be shared, and no excitement at spotting a hawk gliding in the sky. There were, however, several bottles of radiant red cabs lining the pantry. I chose one and uncorked it, filling a long-stemmed wine glass to the rim. Opening the freezer, I decided to pair it with a slightly aged Italian frozen pizza.

After eating, I poured myself a second glass of wine and made my way to the small corridor leading to the three bedrooms at one end of the ranch-style home. Instead of going to the den, I stopped at the door that was adorned with glittering stars in the shape of a heart and a homemade sign that read, *Only Positive People May Enter*. I decided to enter anyway, opening a doorway that led to a time tunnel of sorts. Melissa's room, aglow in shades of pink, was just how she'd left it, and when I say "left," I mean *left this world*. I sat down on her bed, cradling my wine so as not to spill any. It would be a sacrilege to upset anything here. This was no longer a room, but a shrine. There were pictures of Melissa—Mel, as we called her—encircling the space, as well as her Goldfinch watercolors and objects she had growing up, like her favorite blanket, Pokémon, Beanie Babies and the like.

But it was those pictures of her development from a child to pre-adolescent, and from adolescent to young womanhood that always captured me. It was a startling display of human transformation, but maybe a miraculous display is more apt. How could one human have touched and uplifted so many in so brief a time? I was then, and always will be, in awe of her intelligence, a wisdom beyond her years, her smile and of course, her fearlessness.

Certainly, Mel was fearless in the face of death. Right up to the end. Her tender and understanding eyes comforted all of us, especially her fiancé, Samuel, who somehow kept it together despite leaving her hospital room every few minutes to "breathe." Over the last five years of Mel's life, I learned more about acute lymphoblastic leukemia, or *ALL*, than I ever wanted to know. Mostly, I chastised myself for how I had missed the early onset of her symptoms.

Her oncologist once confided in me that I wasn't responsible for not recognizing the initial symptoms of *ALL*, such as fatigue, fever, and even the bruising from playing soccer. Besides, all of these were common symptoms, right? That's only ice-cold consolation for me now. Despite there being no cure, what if we could have added a year, two, or more to her life? I don't think I'll ever forgive myself, no matter what anyone says.

Beth never blamed me, and I don't think she overtly felt angry at me. Whereas Beth had started going to church services again, finding meaning, support and hope in her faith, I just couldn't get onboard the faith-and-redemption train. And so, I never joined her on Sundays, as much as she pleaded for me to come with her. Finally, after a couple of months of trying, she simply stopped asking.

Come to think of it, that was when the web of separation crept in between us, crippling our routine of making meals and sharing our days together. Soon after, Beth had started knitting with a group at the church. Despite my sadness and loneliness,

I'm grateful Beth has found a way to cope with this loss. But unlike her, I'm not so sure I'll ever find a path to healing myself.

I held up a picture of my daughter before she had lost her hair from chemo, with her looking as radiant as ever. Smiling, I kissed the image. "Oh Mel, my sweet, sweet Mel. I'll always love you, Mel," I said before setting it down. In that moment, I broke out of my reverie with the odd sensation that I wasn't sitting in Mel's room alone. A prickly chill ran down my spine. After a few moments, I surmised that it was my own shadow. Not a literal shadow—mind you—but what Jung called "the dark aspects of the personality." How could the good doctor, the one who selflessly helped others, have stood by and watched his own daughter grow ill and not have detected it or acted? How could I have been so damn blind?

When Mel first got sick, as well as during other difficult times, I had always leaned on concepts from mythology and the unconscious mind to help me find balance and escape from the straightjacket of traditional psychotherapy. I strongly believed that a broader, intuitive and less reductionist approach to wellness was something our world badly needed. I was saddened, for example, to find that younger psychotherapists were less inclined to study or invoke Jung, and many courses in counseling theories had stopped teaching him at all.

But the real life-and-death struggles of my only child profoundly changed me, as well as my devotion to anything imaginal, unproven and unscientific. Finally, when the outcome of Mel's illness was incontrovertible, I withdrew into a cave of rationality, where examining potential treatments and measuring outcomes were the only things that mattered.

It wasn't long after Melissa's death that I packed my extensive collection of books on mythology, dreams and archetypes in boxes. Then, on a gray and rainy Saturday, I dropped the books off at a used book store in Old Willamette Village near the house. It was a bittersweet moment. I'd always thought that the universe concealed a profound mystery that we could discern, if only as a fleeting glimpse. That idea, as well as the *kernel of hope* that something existed beyond or after this lifetime, expired when the book shop's rickety door shut behind me.

That's not to say I didn't try to find that *kernel of hope*. I spent nights scouring articles from neuroscientists, hoping to unearth something in our consciousness that would survive death. But article after depressing article perceived the brain in a very mechanistic and reductionist manner, with awareness simply being a by-product of brain activity. According to this glum perspective, free will didn't exist. Everything was determined in a machine-like way that made choice merely an illusion.

Out of desperation, I even sought out information about near death experiences (NDE). Surprisingly, a small number of neurosurgeons and brain scientists had documented their own experiences with near death, claiming that consciousness could not be the result of brain mechanisms, since awareness continued after all brain function had ceased. While these personal anecdotes were compelling, they were almost certainly hallucinations that couldn't be taken seriously in the same way as rigorous scientific study.

Don't get me wrong. I wished that there was some way to transcend our material being, but as I've told my patients more times than I can count, wishing for something doesn't make it so.

Besides, what great mystery, or God, would have deigned to let my lovely Mel lose vitality and disintegrate before my very eyes?

I admit that this train of remorseful thinking, or rumination to be more exact, occurred to me often. Self-loathing and despair were my mind's favorite themes — and not just when spending time in the what I cynically called the *Shrine of Mel*, or Mel's Shrine. I would never think of dismantling the shrine, and besides, Beth would not allow it. But I feared that this memorial, of what was and what could have been, must somehow be

20

transformed if my life with Beth was to move forward.

Have I talked to anyone about my grief, you rightly ask? You've probably heard of that saying, "The physician who treats himself has a fool for a patient." Well, call my reluctance hubris, shame, or what you will, but I know all about the five stages of grief, and once taught a graduate school course that covered it. Besides, who the hell has the right to tell someone like me how to cope? Okay, that's anger, so I guess I'm on stage two.

It was that kind of night until I recalled the sign on the outside of Mel's room. *Only Positive People May Enter.* "Time to go," I thought, tilting the long-stemmed wine glass to finish off the cab. I stood and straightened out the comforter. With one hand on the door knob, I slowly pivoted my head so as to scan the remnants and promise of a life cut short. There wasn't a day that I didn't visit Mel's room, even if for a minute or two. Sometimes, after an especially tough day at the hospital, I even imagined spending time with Mel. We'd have a chat, and her cheery disposition would magically lift my spirits. But tonight? I left her room feeling low and disheartened. I wondered: Could it have something to do with today's new patient, Mason?

Briefly, I stepped into the den to read a recently published journal article about a biological link between pessimism and dementia, but found my thoughts drifting off to the synchronicity of how I'd encountered two so-called "Travelers" in the same afternoon. If there was some deeper meaning here, I couldn't fathom it, and so I decided to prepare for bed, hoping pessimism wasn't frying my brain with Alzheimer's-producing tau and beta amyloid proteins.

I opened the queen-sized pullout sofa bed that I was sure had been designed as a modern day torture device. Once the sheets, pillows and comforter were in place, I made my way to the sliding glass doors in the dining room. But I stopped halfway, seeing that Beth had fallen asleep with her knitting still in her lap. As quietly as possible, I turned off the TV and covered her with the quilt that hung over the back of the sofa.

Outside, the stars were bright, shimmering. One celestial object in the Northwest sky, pulsating with mesmerizing hues of blue, appeared more brightly than any other star. I had the strange thought that it was saying, "Hey look at me! Don't you see me? If you can see me, then I'm not an accident."

That night, lying on the sofa bed with my eyes closed, I could have sworn I saw that bluish star far off in the distance as I slipped into a deep slumber.

Chapter 3

Edward Delabrey adjusted the already perfect knot on his red silk tie. Seeing him in my office reminded me of news reports I'd seen of him during the trial when he had defended the hospital from negligence in the sexual abuse case. He was very tall and solidly built, and he had an imperious expression and a way of looking down at you that was disquieting. He and his wife, Shirley, sat in the two chairs in my office. I positioned myself behind my desk. Given the tense expression on Edward's face, his combative posture and nearly clenched fists, I might need protection. Shirley, on the other hand, was immobile, shoulders stooped, head drooping like a birthday balloon missing half its helium.

"Thank you for coming." I smiled, trying to put Mason's parents at ease. But his father would have none of that.

"What's the plan? What are you going to do for the boy?" His voice was forceful, and I could feel my breath get shallow. I took one intentionally deep breath to stay calm.

"We can't get ahead of ourselves. I'm still talking with Mason. I'm trying to get a better sense of his symptoms so I can make the proper diagnosis."

"He's dangerous, out of control. And what's this about his hearing voices? My wife told me he was talking crazy in the hospital."

"Okay. I think it would help for us to start at the beginning. My purpose today is to understand your family better, and to see what..."

"See what? I don't have all day to sit here without getting this fixed. You know what my hourly rate is? I've got people waiting on me to..."

"Edward," interrupted Shirley without fully looking at her husband. She shifted uncomfortably in her chair and tugged on her beige blouse for no apparent reason as she said weakly, "Maybe we could hear him out." Edward stiffened and glared back, causing Shirley to quickly gaze back down at the floor.

I don't know why, but I suddenly pictured myself setting off the fire alarm at this jerk's office. But I was a professional, and so I continued to explain the process, with a little ego massaging. "We need your help, Mr. and Mrs. Delabrey, because as parents, you know Mason better than anyone. And I can't imagine how trying this whole experience has been for you. Both of you."

Edward eased his posture slightly, even unbuttoning his custom-fitted black suit jacket. His hair was blondish brown, wavy, and meticulously styled so that one long wave hung slightly over his tanned forehead. His jaw was square, and his head held straight up, all of which gave him a commanding appearance. He leaned forward to share, "My eldest son, Edward Jr., was valedictorian of his class in high school. Now he's Phi Beta Kappa in college and star player on the baseball team for OSU. He'll either go into engineering or law. Maybe both. There it is."

I paused, waiting to hear more, but I must have just had a dumbfounded expression on my face.

"What's the matter? I just said it. There it is," repeated Edward, a satisfied and smug look on his face. It was like a final

Chapter 3

summation laid out for an entire life in a couple of sentences.

"I'm sorry, but I don't quite understand your point, Mr. Delabrey."

"My point is this: if one kid is so good, how can the other one be such a lazy screw-up? It's obviously not hereditary. There must be a medication for these, uhm, schizos, or whatever you call them."

"Let's hit the pause button for a moment." I could feel my blood pressure rising. "I never said anything about schizophrenia. I don't have a complete history yet. In any case, I'm glad you mentioned your eldest son. Because when treating anyone, what's important is that we look at the entire family as a dynamic, as a system." I formed the shape of a sphere with my hands, before adding, "And it's not so much as there's anything inherently wrong with Mason. In terms of this approach, he's what we'd call the 'identified patient,' the one in the family who's calling out for help."

"This is bullshit, that's what this is," blurted Edward, his face flushed red as he bolted out of the chair like a missile moving into firing position. "I'm going to talk with Beverly about this."

"You mean Dr. Howell?" I paused as he shot me a disdainful sneer. "Mr. Delabrey, please. This is the standard process we need to go through." I pushed back my chair and stood. By then he was already at the doorway.

"I won't sign anything to release him. Got his own room, doesn't have a job, got all his food and internet paid for, and he's calling out for help because he's what—mistreated? He's a schizo hearing voices, and if I have to file a formal assault charge for what happened two weeks ago to keep him here, I will." Shirley was still seated, ashen, the blood drained from her face.

"Shirl," said Edward loudly as he stepped into the hallway.

Shirley stood up hesitantly. "I'm so sorry. I'll be in touch. I'll tell you whatever you need to know. Mason needs me."

"Yes, he does." All I could do was shake her hand and nod. "Thank you." As I shut the door and sat down to document my meeting with Mason's parents, I thought how often a parent denied what was happening right before them. It was like a car crash in slow motion, and I could understand how Mason's sensitive temperament, when mixed with such a strict, demanding and uncompromising father, created low self-worth and self-esteem. On the one hand, knowing that Edward Delabrey wouldn't be included in future sessions gave me a personal sense of relief. On the other hand, it was important that Edward's refusal to engage in Mason's recovery was not viewed by his son as yet more confirmation that he wasn't worth the effort.

It was another crammed day, with back-to-back patient meetings, staff meetings, and two process groups to run. I'd all but forgotten about Mason until I rushed back to my office at 3:00 pm. Mason was sitting outside the door. He stood up to meet me, tugging on his jeans to keep them up. I noticed his belt had been taken because of suicide safety protocol.

Mason had a little more color in his face. I checked in with him on his hospital experience thus far.

"It's okay. They took my belt. And my shoe laces."

"Yeah, I see. Sorry, but it's just a precaution. How's the food?"

"Kinda sucks."

"Yeah, I was worried about that. Check out the vending machine around the corner from the garden. It's got a better variety of soft drinks, nuts and snacks. Sometimes I use that one." As I spoke, Mason looked around the room, pausing when he got to the bookshelf.

"Go on, take a look. If there's a book you like, you can borrow it."

As Mason perused the bookshelf, I picked up where we left off the previous day, exploring what was going on in his life over the past several months and learning more about his symptoms. As with many patients, I've found it's sometimes easier to relate to and share with them when they are busy doing something else. Mason was fully engaged, especially after he discovered a particular book on my shelf. It was *The Book of Symbols*, which was a collection of over 17,000 images from cultures around the world.

Before I knew it, Mason was sitting on the sofa with the book firmly ensconced in his lap. With eyes open wide and mouth agape, he flipped through the pages as if literally opening himself to receive these images into his very being. While the images flickered by, the story of his life came out. It was like an invisible doorway to the unconscious had opened up, and for as long as the door was open, the flow of information in both directions was unimpeded. So long as Mason held that book in his hands, everything was unfiltered.

Since I had no appointments following Mason's, I let the flow continue, which it did for over an hour. That was the moment Mason shut the book and asked, "Can I really borrow this?"

"Yeah, sure. I know where to find you." I gave him a wink, feeling good about the information I'd gleaned in our session. Given this clearer picture of his past, I was less inclined to diagnose schizophrenia. Firstly, there was no prior history of delusions, hallucinations, disorganized speech, or disorganized behavior lasting longer than a month in duration. There had been only one hallucination with no delusional beliefs accompanying it.

While relationship impairment was included in the constellation of symptoms characterizing schizophrenia, Mason didn't really meet the standard. Yes, he spent a lot of time alone and admitted to having stopped multi-player gaming because he felt it was shallow and manipulative. At the same time, I felt he wasn't being totally forthcoming about his personal relationships, and I hoped that in time he would open up.

Finally, Mason's hostility and aggression could have been viewed as an associated feature of schizophrenia. But now, having the context of meeting his father, I was inclined to put this symptom aside.

From my chart notes:

According to Mason, he and his father engaged in a pushing match over the messiness of his room and his not going to school. Mason reported that when the argument got heated, his father shoved him first. When Mason shoved back, he claimed that his father slipped on a throw rug or piece of clothing, fell back, and slammed his head on the door, temporarily rendering him unconscious. Mason ran for help, but when he and his mother returned, his father shouted that he had one week to "get the hell out of my house."

Mason admitted disliking his father, but said he would never intentionally be violent towards him. The patient claimed that the episode of lighting fireworks in a stairwell to set off a fire alarm was an attempt to embarrass his father and interrupt his work. Mason now agreed that it backfired and was "totally the wrong way" to make a point.

I was convinced that Mason's symptoms much more likely fit the criteria for a major depressive episode, and that was the diagnosis code I entered. He met several of the criteria, including having depressed, sad and hopeless feelings for over three months. He had lost pleasure in and stopped participating in activities he once liked. He experienced sleeplessness, as well as fatigue. Finally, he had feelings of worthlessness. The suicidal thoughts had occurred spur of the moment and were not premeditated. In fact, he was well aware that his mother had an appointment which—had it not been canceled unbeknownst to him—would have had her coming into the garage to get the car, thus discovering him much earlier.

This led me to believe that the suicide attempt was actually a call for help. At the gut level, this felt right. It clarified my treatment for Mason, but might mean transferring him elsewhere, where the level of care was less intensive. By the end of the session, my formulation for how to work with Mason had coalesced and was ready to be shared.

"Mason, here's what I'm thinking for your treatment," I said, making sure I had his attention. I then explained that I would start him on the antidepressant fluoxetine at 10 mg, to be increased to 20 mg if well tolerated. Other treatments would consist of family sessions with his mother, art therapy group, and group process sessions focusing on emotions. I'd try and work with him as often as possible one-on-one. He agreed to the overall plan, then asked some follow-up questions about the medication's side effects. I told him that if there were any side effects that they usually showed up right away, and we could always switch to another medication.

"Mason, we're out of time today. How about we plan for you to come in again tomorrow?"

"Dr. Banks?" he said as he opened the door.

"What?"

"I saw him again last night." Mason nonchalantly brushed his hair away from his eyes.

"Saw who?"

"The Traveler."

Before I could utter a word in response, Mason had already scuttled out the door, clutching *The Book of Symbols* in his hand.

Chapter 4

The next morning was a blur. At the daily staff meeting, I listened as the other clinicians presented their cases. Dr. Beverly always leaned forward slightly, poised hawk-like, as if waiting for a vulnerable prey. Whenever the clinician was done, Dr. Beverly made a beeline directly to any potential issue in need of fixing. I was convinced that Beverly went home and spent her evenings studying psychological research and the latest scientifically proven modalities. She seemed especially enamored of "evidence-based" therapy (EBT) approaches like Dialectical Behavior Therapy (DBT), Cognitive Behavioral Therapy (CBT), and others. Typically, these evidence-based programs were based on a manual, or rigid set of teachings, that had been shown to be effective in peer-reviewed studies. While I saw value in these programs, particularly in group settings like our clinic, their one-size-fits all, paint-by-numbers approach felt one-dimensional and unsatisfying.

Finally, my turn came, and I presented Mason's diagnosis and plan. After explaining why I ruled out schizophrenia, Dr. Beverly asked a few pointed questions about the assault, which I answered by giving my impression of Edward Delabrey, along with the likelihood he might be verbally, if not physically, abusive for having shoved his son.

"Dr. Banks, that's a dangerous and irresponsible charge to make without a shred of proof. I strongly caution you against making these kinds of accusations."

I was taken aback at her strong defense of Edward Delabrey, but she was right that I lacked any evidence, other than Mason's word. "Okay, I can see that," I conceded with a nod.

Beverly continued, "If his father's going to be a problem, you'll want to document any changes in Mason's behavior that could affect the diagnosis. Even the slightest ones. Still, given the patient's symptoms, the diagnosis of schizophrenia seems reasonable."

Dr. Rick chimed in, "It's pretty clear that the boy meets criteria. You said he's isolated, relationship impaired, hearing things, violent. Plus, his age of onset concurs with the research about schizophrenia." I felt like he was just piling on.

"Not quite, Rick. Just give me a little more time. I have a feeling about it," I countered, looking at Beverly.

"Okay, but I don't want to regret this," she answered with pursed lips.

I decided not to mention Mason's disclosure to me about seeing "the Traveler" again. That disclosure, by the way, was right out of the patient playbook. It was what I preferred to call the "one hand on the doorknob revelation"—a bombshell shared by patients just as they were walking out the door. In Mason's case, it was a parting gift to ruin my evening, a verbal grenade that threatened to blow up my entire diagnosis and treatment plan.

While a second episode of hearing voices or seeing someone imaginary was troubling, it still didn't exactly meet the "at least a one-month period" minimum requirement for schizophrenia according to standards of the Diagnostic and Statistical Manual, also known as the DSM. While I never liked pathologizing anyone, diagnostic codes were necessary for insurance billing purposes.

Mason was scheduled on my appointment planner for two meetings that day. The first was with his mother for a family session. When she entered the room, Shirley gave Mason a long hug. She wore black pants and a dark gray patterned blouse, almost as if she were attending a funeral. She rubbed her son's back, and then kissed him on the cheek. Looking directly at him, she asked how he was doing. Mason just lowered his head and mumbled "K."

"Do you have enough clothes? What about shoes? Are these your only shoes?" she said, looking down at his worn athletic shoes.

"I'm good, Mom," he muttered with a strong tinge of embarrassment.

"No, I'm buying you a new pair of walking shoes. You need good shoes."

When Mason sat down on the sofa, Shirley quickly took a seat beside him, assuming an upright posture, as if forcing herself to hold it together despite the gravity of the situation. Mason's body language was such that he leaned slightly toward his mother. He was wearing jeans and a dark brown T-shirt.

When I introduced the idea of understanding the family and how it operated, Shirley starting wringing her hands. She also tugged on her diamond studded wedding ring, pulling it off and on her finger, then twirling it around. If this was a symbolic expression, and I often think such things are, she was wrestling with her marriage. I also noticed how the corrugator and glabellar muscles around her forehead and eyes were tightly drawn, as were the muscles around her mouth and lips, causing a frowning expression. She was under obvious duress and almost certainly depressed. The application of bright makeup on her cheeks and around her puffy eyes seemed poor compensation for the truth of her mood and the fact that she had been crying. I noted her facial expression in my notes.

My style as a therapist is to point out what's working, and then to build on that. I began with a short psycho-educational description of families as a system that can be healthy, or dysfunctional, and have blind spots. In this context, no one in the family was really separate from the parts. Then, I suggested that one place to start would be to look at what was working in the family.

Mason shrank into his seat, as if gravity had increased its pull by at least 2 Gs or more. Shirley forced a smile and jumped in by telling what a good provider her husband was, and how he was always there when the family needed him. Mason made a huffing sound under his breath.

"Mason? Were you going to say something?"

"Yeah. If he's so good, then where is he?" asked Mason, his eyes on fire. "I thought this was a family meeting."

"Shirley, I think Mason has a valid point." I said this calmly, aligning with Mason. "Maybe you can explain why your husband didn't join us."

Shirley blinked several times as if she had some dust in her eye. After a few moments she spoke haltingly, "I asked him to come, but he... he has meetings all week. We thought maybe it would be better if just I went. He cares about you, Mason."

"He's an asshole who only cares about his membership in the Yacht Club and being a big shot when he drives up in his Mercedes."

"That's not true. He only wants the best for you, Mason. Didn't he offer to get you a car?"

"Why's it always about the *stuff*?" Mason's eyes narrowed as he glared at his mother. "It's always about the fucking *stuff*, isn't it?"

"He wanted you to apply to college. That's not about stuff."

"Right, so long as I get the hell out of the house. He didn't even come to see me in the hospital."

Shirley bit her lip as a dark veil seemed to descend over her. As hard as the silence was to tolerate, I let it continue. Finally, I interrupted and asked that we all take a couple of long breaths to regain presence and emotional control.

"So from what I'm hearing, the family operates quite well on the level of material goods, but maybe not so smoothly in the emotional goods department? There's a lot of pain here. I have to say, that if *I'd* attempted suicide, and the one person in the world who I wanted to show up and let me know I was loved *didn't* show up, I'd be horribly hurt and betrayed. And maybe, unforgivably pissed off and angry?"

I watched them both. Mason's forehead wrinkled, as if some new idea or insight was attempting to force its way inside. Further, I explained that families were complex, carrying the history of their ancestors, and often reliving the unresolved trauma. "After all, what more does anyone really want but to be loved and affirmed by their family."

Shirley started to sniffle. Soon, the sniffle turned into a full-blown cry with tears mixing with eyeliner and blush. I leaned over from my chair and handed her a box of tissues. Through the tears, she proceeded to take all the blame for the family's current problems, which didn't really surprise me.

She described how she had gotten married in college to escape an alcoholic and violent home where her mother and older brothers were routinely beaten by her father. Shirley shared that there was even a time when "living in that house," that she felt like killing herself. While Shirley steadfastly denied that her husband had ever physically abused her, she blamed herself for not doing a better job of protecting her children, especially Mason. "He was always special, he was different." Finally, Shirley admitted that she never shared these secrets because, "I was frozen by the burden of shame and guilt." The entire time, Mason winced, head askew, looking at his mother out of the corner of his eyes.

After sitting in silence for a long moment, I asked Mason what it was like to learn about his mother's history and the hardships she'd endured. He averted his gaze from his mother until finally, he caught his breath and spoke.

"So Gdad is some kind of abusive psycho? That's great. I guess being fucked up runs in the family."

"I'd be surprised if you felt any other way." My empathetic tone was meant to affirm and normalize Mason's statement. I doubted anyone in his life did that for him. Then I continued, "So there's that, the history, and how does it make you feel to hear this?"

"Shitty," answered Mason.

"Well, shitty is *kind of* an emotion. How else might you describe it? As making you feel sad, shamed, angry? Take your time."

"*Really* shitty. Really, really, really shitty."

It was near the end of our time, so I explained how it wasn't just the shame and humiliation of the family's secrets that were debilitating, but the consuming guilt over not doing something about it.

"Children trapped in such circumstances beyond their control are naturally conflicted about the abusing parent. As hurt as they are, they'll always have a deep attachment to their parent, and a need to be loved." I hoped my concluding words created a link of understanding between mother and son. On the way out, Shirley and Mason hugged one another. I thanked them both for their courage, before letting them know we'd meet again next week.

Chapter 5

I'd packed an egg salad sandwich, almonds and a banana for lunch, which I brought to a favorite bench outside in the courtyard. From here, I could see all three wings of the hospital, the substance abuse clinic, the adult psychiatric clinic, and the forensic clinic. The forensic clinic stood out for the black wrought iron burglar bars covering the windows. Except, these bars were installed for keeping potentially violent patients in, not keeping burglars out.

I made a point not to take my phone with me, so I could have a few minutes in peace to recharge. Usually, I enjoyed the scenery, but today my attention was drawn to an unseemly blackberry bush, replete with thorns, which grew out from between two poorly manicured shrubs. I noticed several other plants that were growing wildly. This overgrowth was unacceptable for our long-time gardener, Reggie, who lived alone in a small cottage on the property. Though getting up in years, that never stopped him from keeping everything looking picture perfect.

Often, when I was having lunch outside, Reggie would stop by with a handful of blueberries from the clinic's own bushes. "Here, Doc, fresh from the psych farm," kidded Reggie, his straight gray hair flopping gently on his forehead as he spoke. He always wore a pair of denim overalls with gardening tools stuck in the belt and pockets. Each week he brought fresh cut flowers into the waiting room or activities room to cheer up patients, and he was never without a smile or kind word. Once, when I asked why he'd stayed with us for so long, he just grinned. "Who else would have me? At least here I don't have to be committed." Another time, when I commented how he lived like a monk, he guffawed and punched me lightly on the arm. "Well, I kind of like it that way, which is why no woman would have me!"

One day, seemingly out of character, Reggie joined me on the bench, and with a serious expression divulged to me he'd been married to "the best, sweetest woman in the world, Liz." They were young when Liz died in a boating accident, and Reggie decided to remain single. "After perfection, you can't do any better can you?!" he exclaimed. As it turned out, I learned that it was the anniversary of the day she passed, and he had made a small flower shrine on the grounds that only I knew about. That was Reggie.

I decided to check on him, and after I finished lunch, I trekked over to the one-room stone cottage that stood nearly camouflaged beneath the low hung branches of a massive and meandering oak. I followed the quaint, uneven stone path that led to the door. I knocked and there was no answer. I looked in the window, but couldn't make anything out. Back in the clinic, I asked Fran if she'd seen, "Reggie the Gardener," as he was sometimes referred to.

"Nope. He usually brings us some flowers for the vases," she said, motioning to two decorative plastic vases sans blooms.

In the cafeteria, I disposed of my brown bag in the recycling bin. When I saw our Executive Director, Beverly, I asked if she had spoken to Reggie. She just stared at me like she'd seen a ghost.

"Oh my goodness. You don't know?"

"Know what?"

"Reggie passed away. Must have been two months ago."

For a moment I was without words. Finally, a few words tumbled out. "What, what happened? How did he..."

"Not sure, really. I think they found him one day in the cottage. I heard it was a heart attack."

"Two months?"

"I'm sorry no one informed you. We should have notified staff, but we were under a crunch with the Joint Commission being here." Her point hit home, because there wasn't a hospital in Oregon that didn't fear oversight by the Joint Commission, whose examiners could shut you down in a heartbeat for any number of violations. She continued, explaining, "We tried to find his family, but unfortunately we couldn't locate any. So we just had the coroner take the body. I promise I'll notify all staff today, okay? I don't know what else..."

I just stood there, trying to move. But I couldn't.

"Ben. Ben, you all right?" Beverly asked, stepping closer to me, but I just stumbled silently outside.

How could she say, "We tried to find his family," because weren't *we* his family? And if not us, then who? Most of all, I realized my own complicity in this event, steeped in my own ignorance and blindness. I'd taken all these mindfulness trainings and always preached to colleagues and patients that "we need to be mindful." And yet, they'd carted off his body without a memorial, and I never noticed that this kind man, who blessed us with his constant smiles come rain or shine, with his funny stories, his flowers and blueberries, with his *pureness of heart*, had gone missing.

I sat in that garden from late August almost every day, and I didn't think a thing of not seeing him? Would I have noticed if he'd been dead for six months or a year even? Yep, that's mister mindful for you. Totally checked out and not even knowing it.

I was furious with myself and filled with sorrow for the loss of Reggie, who I considered a true friend. What really hit me was when I thought about what might have been different if I *had* been paying attention.

ATTENTION, for Goddamn's sake!

Such was the dark mindset of self-reproach that I carried with me into my individual session with Mason that afternoon.

Chapter 6

Mason stepped slowly inside the office, not making eye contact. After taking a seat, I began my follow-up to check on his medication, which he had started the day before. But instead of being engaging like he'd been in previous sessions—even during his family meeting earlier that day—his affect was flat, and he was speaking in monotone with monosyllabic answers.

"Did you start on the fluoxetine?"

"Yeah."

"Did you experience any side effects like I talked about?"

"Nah."

"I see you went to Art Therapy today. What can you tell me about it?"

"Was okay."

"What kind of activities did you do there?"

"I dunno."

"I mean, did you draw or create anything? Meet anyone?"

"No."

"Mason, what's going on? What are you feeling? Does this have anything to do with the meeting earlier with your mother?"

"No."

"What do you think it's about, then?"

"The world sucks."

"It sucks." I opened my file cabinet and found a file folder titled "Feelings." I pulled out a page and shut the drawer.

"Yeah, and while I was in the hospital my father was at his law firm protecting all those greedy assholes who are burning a hole in the atmosphere."

"You know, I'm really sorry he didn't show up for you. *That* sucks." I nodded at him, sensing a heaviness in my heart. "You know, Mason, sometimes it helps to identify our feelings more clearly. This is a feelings chart." I handed him a sheet of paper filled with over 70 different feelings from ashamed, apathetic and anxious to embarrassed, skeptical, confused and playful.

"What good will this do?"

"Well, think of it as increasing your emotional vocabulary. Research shows that when we're more in touch with our feelings, that we're actually calmer, in control and able to make changes. Otherwise, our feelings can jerk us around. That make sense?"

"Guess so."

"See if you can start noticing your moods a little more. You might be surprised how often they change. And that's normal. Just take a look, okay?"

"Okay," he said, folding the feelings chart and placing it beside him.

"Almost forgot. Your sister, Dilly, called. She wants to visit you."

"Dr. Banks, is being here really going to change anything? Will this make a difference when I go back home?"

"Hopefully, we're going to figure all that out. In time." I let out a sigh, a nonverbal transition of sorts. "Mason, do you know what a fighter pilot is taught to do when their plane is surrounded by enemy fire?" Since we're talking about emotions here, I should mention that Mason shot me a look that fell somewhere between being extremely pissed off and bewildered.

I pretended not to notice and continued, "Well, they're trained to do the next thing. The one thing necessary to keep them in the air until they can land safely. That means they don't think about the future or the past. They are totally focused on getting through the crisis. That's what I'd like us to do in our work. Let's get you feeling better and thinking in ways that are helpful to you."

"How long will that take?"

"Depends. But once you're feeling better, we can have those discussions about moving forward in your life and what to do. You have a lot of strengths, Mason, some of which you probably never thought of." I smiled, thinking that now would be the perfect time to lay the groundwork for exploring strengths, as used in positive psychology. But that was before Mason derailed my plans.

"Hard to be positive when my dad calls me a 'loser.'"

Can a patient hear when a therapist mentally says, "Oh shit"? Good thing they can't because *Oh shit* is what happens every time you're about to move in a direction, and then the patient forces you to change course. Truth be told, a quick thought flashed through my head that maybe Mason would be better served by first focusing on distress-tolerance skills in sessions, as well as in a Dialectical Therapy Behavior therapy group, which consisted of several modules taught in a group setting. But Mason's statement offered an opportunity to maintain continuity and build on our earlier discussion about feelings. I asked Mason to look at the feelings chart and describe his feelings about his father's rigidity.

"What do you mean?"

I offered the example of his father's insistence upon his attending university to get a business or other worthwhile degree. "How does that make you feel?"

Perhaps for the first time, Mason identified feelings such as "inadequate," "rejected," "inferior," "insignificant," and "sad."

He seemed almost surprised to have found these words, and it gave him a greater understanding of his narrative, his life story. Then, I tried to frame this in an even bigger picture. "It's hard for anyone to face their father's rejection. It's easy to feel like a disappointment, even when you're not. This feeling of rejection from a father happens to a lot of men. Maybe we can talk more about what that feels like?"

Mason shared more about his father's desire for him to attend a prestigious, private school. Mason, however, had little interest in traditional schooling. Because of this, his father demeaned him as a "loser" and a "loner" and "worthless." According to Mason, his father had never attended any school event where his artistic projects were prominently displayed. Even after winning a first-place award for his print engravings, his father had declared it, "a meaningless joke for those who can't succeed in real school."

Though I felt my heart drop, I conveyed how successful artists and the artistic process were often misunderstood. While this gave me some ideas for working with Mason individually, I knew deep down there would be no easy path to cultivating a mutually caring and forgiving relationship between Mason and his father. I could have continued on the father-son dynamic, but a glance at the clock made me realize there was only time to investigate Mason's "doorknob revelation" from the day before.

"Mason, the next time we meet, I'd like to learn more about your artwork, okay? Maybe you could bring something in? But first, I wanted to talk about what you told me the other day. About seeing the Traveler? Remember?"

"It was so real. The Traveler appeared to me like before, only this time I was lying in bed."

"Were you sleeping?"

"No, I don't think so. I was just lying there when I saw him. He was wearing a black cloak with a hood. His arm reached out and touched the side of my head. Right here," he said, tapping his left temple.

"Then what happened? Did the Traveler say anything?"

"It was weird. He asked me a short question about someone whose name I didn't know. But I didn't have any kind of answer. Then he stepped forward and hugged me. At first, I was afraid... but all of a sudden, I was surrounded in light and felt myself lifting up really fast. Before I knew it, I was floating in the sky. It was so easy to move around. I remember looking down and seeing the Willamette River. It was so cool to see it from above, in the dark. We followed the river all the way to the Clackamas River above the Oregon City Falls."

"We? Who's 'we'?" I interrupted.

"The Traveler, at least I think that's who I was following. He was in front of me. When he moved in a direction, so did I. Finally, he went down to the Old Willamette area. We were cruising low, just above the houses not far from the river. Then, he stopped in front of this one house, I can't tell you the color because it was dark. But for some reason I was drawn inside and went in alone."

"What did you see?"

"The TV was on. And there was this lady asleep on a purple couch in the living room. She was knitting something, and there was a pile of yarn on her lap."

Listening to Mason, my throat tightened. I tried, but couldn't swallow. I sipped from the cup of tea on the side table next to my chair.

He continued, "Then I knew, that the Traveler's question was connected with this house."

"What was the question?"

"Oh yeah. That's the weird thing. He just said, 'Who's Mel?' That's all the Traveler said to me. 'Who's Mel?'"

Could he mean *my Mel*? Involuntarily, my eyes darted around my office looking for anything that could have given away this breach of confidentiality. I had long ago removed any personal photos from my office.

"So, I think I'm supposed to ask the owner of that house about Mel."

"Well, that's just not possible, Mason," I replied, my speech rapid and under pressure.

"But I saw it."

"What I mean is, it was probably a dream state."

"But it was real. As real as everything in this room."

"Well then, do you remember any other details? Things about the house that could verify where you were? Like specific colors or objects?" I asked, trying to convince myself that Mason's description was nothing more than the kind of hypnogogic hallucinogenic experience that many people report having between waking and falling asleep.

Mason's brow furrowed and his eyes traveled upwards to retrieve his memories. "I remember the yarn on her lap was definitely pink. And there was a photograph on the side table next to her of a girl, maybe 18 or 19, very pretty with brown hair down to about here." He raised his hand just above his shoulder. "Wait. Just a minute!" His eyes got intense, like a television detective putting together what seemed like disconnected clues. "The picture frame was shaped to make the letter M. That couldn't be Mel, could it? Mel's a guy's name."

"Uh huh, usually." As I answered, I could feel my hands tightening their grip on the armrest of my chair.

Mason looked around the room. Suddenly, his gaze fixated on an object in the corner. I swiveled my head to look. There, on a small stand nestled behind the door rested my briefcase. "Mason, what is it?"

"That old briefcase. It's just like the one in the house, on the purple sofa with the lady. It had the same UO sticker in the corner... exactly like this one."

The distinctive yellow and green sticker of the University of Oregon was ubiquitous around town, but not when placed on a worn brown briefcase resting on the edge of a purple sofa. I sat there motionless. Speechless.

"Wait. And there was this man sitting alone in a room. I remember floating above him for just a second. He was holding a glass of wine."

In disbelief, I recalled the distinct feeling I'd had of being watched that night in Melissa's room. Wide-eyed and baffled, I could only stare at Mason, who once more surveyed the briefcase and then looked back at me.

"You mean... that's *your* house?" asked Mason. My mind could not make sense of what I was hearing. My belief systems about science and reality collided with the impossibility before me. For a time, and I'm not sure how long, I must have gone somewhere. I'm not sure where—maybe it was the "safe place" I was always telling patients to find for themselves when they were negatively triggered or felt threatened.

Anyway, at some point I finally felt myself shaking, or being shaken. A muffled voice far off in the distance got louder and louder until I could make out words, "Dr. Banks! Dr. Banks, are you all right!?"

My body shuddered, and I realized Mason was holding my arm and shaking me awake from what I can only describe as a temporary catalepsy.

"I'm sorry, but I was worried. You weren't moving or saying anything."

"Uhm, how long was I like that?" I was embarrassed asking him, but needed to know.

"A few minutes. I don't know, maybe five."

"Five minutes... Jesus!" I glanced around the room trying to get my bearings.

"I was just about to go for help."

"No, no, no. I'm okay now, thanks," I smiled weakly. "It's just that... what you said."

"Dr. Banks?—Who's Mel?"

I felt a wave, no, a thundering tsunami of emotion engulf me. This wounded part of my life and all the emotions that I'd hidden away and kept out of my work hit me. My head dropped into my hands. My defenses fell away. All the things that I was taught as a therapist about separating roles and confidentiality seemed irrelevant in the moment. I was here in my own suffering — very un-therapist like — with a young man, also suffering. We were just two souls trying to find hope and make sense out of things. I looked up at Mason, my eyes moist and chest heaving. That's when I did the unthinkable.

"I wish you could have met her, Mason. Mel was my daughter. Melissa. She died not too long ago. And sometimes I think, if I can just help one person, then maybe it will be worthwhile. That I can go on living, because..." my voice fluttered, and Mason kindly touched my shoulder and handed me my teacup. I took a short sip, continuing, "because I know that would have made her happy. That's just the kind of person she was."

Mason picked up a box of tissues and handed it to me. I blew my nose, straightened up and composed myself. As Mason looked at me, I had the odd impression that he was much wiser than his age. Immediately, I felt embarrassed and compelled to restore my role as the therapist in the room. I immediately apologized for sharing personal information, also firmly stating that the session was about *him*, and *definitely not me*. Truth be told, all I wanted to do was to get him out of the room so I could process my own thoughts and feelings.

I thanked Mason for sharing his experience and said that we'd pick up talking about his art and his strengths in our next meeting. Mason paused in the doorway and turned to me with a very serious expression on his face.

"Dr. Banks?

"Yes?"

"Tonight, maybe you should go home and chill, okay?"

"Yeah, right. Thanks, good idea." I forced a chuckle and

ushered him out the door. My chart notes totally omitted any mention of the Traveler and Mason's apparent viewing of my house. I knew this omission wasn't really proper, but I couldn't wrap my head around it. It didn't qualify as a hallucination because Mason didn't see anything that wasn't really there. I'd save my analysis of that for later, after I did some research at home. With that, I shut down my computer.

As I reached for my briefcase, a splash of yellow caught my eye. There, on the sill outside my window stood an American Goldfinch, Mel's favorite bird, showing off its bright, sun-drenched yellow body. As I leaned forward for a closer look, the bird's small black wings fluttered twice, and then it chirped at me, or so it seemed. It cocked its jet-black cap covered head to the side while making eye contact with me.

We looked at each other in this way for how long I cannot say. Then, in what seemed like no more than a millisecond, the little yellow bird hopped once and took flight, disappearing from view.

Chapter 7

I was just about to shut my office door when the phone rang. I almost let it go to voicemail, but picked up, wondering if it might be a late cancelation. But no, it was Shirley Delabrey, who asked, in a hushed voice, if she could see me alone. When I asked if it could wait until our family meeting on Thursday, she said no, insisting that it was necessary for us to meet as soon as possible. The next day was filled, so I offered to see her before my morning staff meeting. Speaking barely above a whisper, Shirley thanked me before hanging up. Instantly, my mind starting whirring away, turning the hamster wheel of reasons why this meeting felt so *sub rosa*.

In fact, I was so wrapped up thinking about Shirley's call that I almost didn't hear our receptionist, Fran, say "goodnight." She repeated my name several times until I turned to face her. Fran's scarlet colored horn-rimmed glasses matched the tightly curled ringlets of red hair that dangled and danced beside her head each time she spoke.

"Huh?" I blurted.

"Dr. Banks, is everything okay?"

"Sorry?"

51

"You seemed preoccupied. I didn't mean to bother you."

"No, Fran. You're right. I was lost in my thoughts."

"Well, like my mother always told me, 'You're allowed,'" she said with a chuckle.

"Fran, did you see the note Dr. Howell sent out today about Reggie?"

"Oh, yes. So sad. I can't believe he's gone."

"I want to plan a memorial service for him in the chapel. Is that something you'd be interested in coming to?"

"Yes, definitely. He was such a sweet man. So funny, too."

"I agree. I'll let you know when. And, now officially, 'Goodnight Fran.'" I took off my hat and bowed slightly, as an aristocrat might.

"Goodnight, my good sir." Fran giggled and playfully performed a partial curtsy from behind her desk.

Outside, the sky was covered in gray and the air suffused in a light drizzle. "Must be Halloween time, that's when the rains start," I thought to myself as I opened the green wrought iron gate to the street. Instead of going to my car, I stood and gazed at the garden, which was already looking woeful and unkempt since Reggie's departure. That's when I saw a figure hunched beside a large maple tree, the red-brown leaves still hanging on and providing a bit of shelter. As I moved closer for a better look, a small dog dashed out from the tree, tail wagging. Excitedly, it jumped up to greet me, wet paws splattering my pants.

"Bear, no!" shouted a strangely familiar voice.

I looked up and saw the woman with the dog who I had bumped into a few days earlier. She quickly approached and pointed at Bear, who obediently sat down. "He knows better. Sorry he got you all wet. You know what they say, 'Must be Halloween time, that's when the rains start.'" She winked slyly at me, just like before. I furrowed my brow. How in the world did she do that? This was the second time she seemed to know my thoughts. Like *exactly*.

"Traveler Jacki, right?"

"You remembered my name," she grinned.

"Hey, I thought you and Bear were getting on a train for somewhere warm. Everything okay?"

"Know how sometimes you got a plan, but then you find a better plan? So me and Bear, we is just stickin' around. Maybe find some work in exchange for a place to stay." Traveler Jacki's light green eyes glimmered hopefully.

I scratched my head, trying to sell myself on the idea that I was trying to think of places they might stay for the night, like local shelters, rooms, or churches. Problem was, I didn't know any.

"Sorry to hear about your gardener friend. Who'll take care of the flowers and garden now?"

"Huh? How in heaven's name could you know what happened to Reggie? Only the hospital knows that."

"Well, no, I don't know nuthin'. It's just that when me and Bear was here before, the flowers looked happy. Now they're looking real sad, like they lost someone very close, don't they?"

"Yeah. Well, come to think of it, they do look pretty sad. Reggie really loved this garden." I was speechless for a moment, considering that there must be more to this woman and her dog than meets the eye. "Hey, wait." I paused to consider the possibility of offering them a ride. But my concern about professional liability vetoed that idea rather quickly. "Actually, I think I do know a place," I said, raising my hand to point the way. "I remember seeing a shelter or hostel just off 26th. I drive by there all the time." Before I could offer directions, Traveler Jacki impishly interrupted.

"Ben, you work here, huh?" She pointed to the clinic's sign, which stood a good ten feet above the ground, over the gated entryway.

"Uh, yeah?" I responded suspiciously.

"This hospital, who's in there? What kinda people?"

"If you mean patients, it's a psychiatric hospital, residential. Anyway, like I was saying, to get to the shelter you have to go down..."

"No, wait!" Traveler Jacki suddenly kneeled down and began rummaging through her backpack. In the last minute, the sky had opened up to produce what was now a heavy rainstorm. Water funneled off my leather fedora and into my face. The next thing I knew, she shoved a packet of papers at me.

"Here. Take these. Explains everything."

"Look, I'm sorry." I raised both hands high in the air, palms open, like double stop signs. "I don't get what this is about."

"You will, Ben. Bless you!" She grabbed my arms, pulling them down and putting the papers directly into my hands. I had never met a salesperson who was this persistent, yet made me want to smile at the same time.

"I can't see. Wait a sec." I blinked water out of my eyes, trying to have a look. My glasses had fogged up, so I took my glasses off and tried to rub them clean with my thumb, creating a spectacular array of light-bending swirly marks on the lenses. "I'm sorry," I pleaded, taking my glasses off again.

"We'll be in touch!" Then, in one deft move, she swept Bear into her arms and scampered out the front gate and across the street.

"Wait! Your papers! What do I do with these? How will I find you?!" I shouted over the thrumming rain. I readjusted my hat's outer frame to divert the raindrops, desperately trying to see where she and Bear had gone. Finally, I stuffed the papers under my jacket to keep them from getting drenched.

Moments later, windshield wipers pumping furiously and defroster on full blast, my car crawled around the block where I had seen Traveler Jacki and Bear only seconds before. For the second time, they had disappeared right before my eyes, and I could only turn toward home. I wasn't sure how I could help them, but tonight, there were more pressing issues to consider.

Chapter 7

When I pulled up to the driveway, light silvery smoke curled up from the chimney. It was a sign of life, the first wood burning fire of the year, which I was glad to see. The green tarp covering a cord of alder wood near the back of the house was untied. Inside, Beth had stacked freshly cut alder by the fireplace, filling the house with the woodsy smell of the forest. Still carrying my briefcase, I walked over to the photo of Mel on the side table. The letter M-shaped frame was undeniable.

"Do you mind if I move this picture to the other side table?"

"Why?"

"It's easier for me to see from there. If that's okay."

"Sure," she nodded, adding a shrug like a punctuation mark.

Impulsively, I sat down on the couch, as close as I could without crushing her box of yarn. She stopped knitting, surprised.

"Beth... I..." I looked at her as thoughts flooded me. There was so much I had held in since Mel's death. I wanted so badly to share our lives again, but my awkwardness didn't help.

"Um, thanks for making the fire. Smells really nice."

Beth ever so gently reached out and placed her hand on top of mine. She didn't hold my hand so much as touch it in shared sympathy. It was a sign of our missing one another, and I could feel my eyes welling up. Hers did too. For a flicker of a moment, I thought we might talk about our feelings. Or just anything, even the mundane.

"In time, Ben. In time," whispered Beth before returning to her knitting. I gulped hard and stood up. Our small exchange didn't really change anything, but I guessed she was right. Still, it felt good to gaze into her large brown eyes, to drink in her kind countenance, soft lips and peach skin tones. I wanted nothing more in that moment than to pull her close and hold her like we used to hold one another.

I repositioned Mel's photo to the other end table. If Mason really could remote-view our home, then he could verify it by noting changes like this one. As an additional test, I carried my briefcase into my office rather than set it on the edge of the sofa like I normally did.

I had no dinner except for chips and cheese. Then I poured myself a tall glass of cabernet in preparation for a night of study and I hoped, discovery. To tell you the truth, having a laser focus energized me and reminded me of the all-nighters I pulled during my medical school residency at a run-down emergency department on Chicago's north side, not too far from Wrigley Field. Since I had donated all my books on Jungian dreamwork, I found an old dream journal that I hoped would give me some clues for deciphering how Mason's experience might be understood through the workings of the unconscious mind.

Eventually, I conceptualized how to make more sense of Mason's experience—without falling prey to unproven beliefs about the occult. Personally, the occult made me think about spiritualists like the Russian occultist Madame Blavatsky and others popular in the nineteenth and twentieth centuries. The key to understanding what had happened, I thought, was contextual. Instead of taking it literally, what if Mason's dream of flying was viewed as a vivid waking dream?

In that way, it could be about escaping or rising above the oppressiveness of life as experienced on the ground and in a body. A pilot, even if the pilot is directing one's own body, could be pictured as an attempt to control one's destiny—especially when things are so out of control. Flight represented freedom, the ability or desire to be free and independent, which fit for someone of Mason's age. He wanted to pilot his own life, but was woefully unprepared. And so, his imagination took him up and into the light.

Then there was the light, which as I saw it, signified the repression of his shadow side—perhaps the repressed anger he felt toward his father. Instead of facing the shadow of his ego, he was avoiding and dissociating from this part of himself. Yes. Suddenly, it made perfect sense.

Until it made no sense. Maybe utter non-sense.

A wave of uncertainty flooded over me. How would this help me treat him anyway? Even if there was some truth to these aspects of his unconscious mind, they merely seemed to lead me into a rabbit hole filled with more questions than answers. I needed concrete answers, not concepts. Nonetheless, the idea of piloting his own life and entering the light were metaphors that might prove helpful. Now, if I could translate that into action, into skills that he needed, he might eventually learn to take control over his own mind and life, which was now in a tailspin.

When I glanced up at the metal clock on the wall, I was surprised to find that it was half past midnight. I sighed, hopeful that maybe my long evening of study would yet bear some fruit. At least, I mused, there would be less time spent on my gulag-inspired pull-out bed.

I brushed my teeth and climbed onto the sofa bed. Lying in the dark, my mind was still active. I'd spent hours scouring old notes, searching the internet for clues, and while at the symbolic level I could understand Mason's traveler experiences as an archetypal mechanism driving his psyche and imagination, Mason didn't enact his imagination. He *literally* saw my house and specific objects in it.

Just then an odd thought occurred to me—had he somehow used clairvoyance to conjure up a visual imagery of scenes? I remembered reading how Sigmund Freud felt threatened by one of his most brilliant students, Victor Tausk, who was uncannily able to anticipate Freud's ideas and flesh them out even more quickly than the great master himself. Maybe Mason had tapped into my mind to get his information? Memories flooded me of the time when, as a college student, I was drawn to the mystical realm by reading Castaneda, Huxley and Hesse, not to mention dabbling in hallucinogens. These all hinted of a vivid reality that coexisted with the material world. My medical school training, however, put an end to these explorations.

The image of Traveler Jacki popped into my head. It was eerie how she seemed to know my thoughts almost verbatim. "Oh crap," I thought. I'd totally forgotten about the papers she had given me earlier that day. I didn't want to get out of bed, but figured it was best to have a look.

I flipped on the lights and sat at the vintage oak roll-top desk I had found at an antique shop. The papers were still damp, stuck together in a briefcase pocket where I'd stuffed them. After a bit of flattening, they were still crumpled, but at least legible. The front page had an official stamp and said something about "Registration."

A little closer examination let me discover something I never could have guessed. It seemed that Traveler Jacki and Bear might have a new plan in place after all. That is, if I could ever find them again.

Chapter 8

Outside the nurses' station, an orderly rolled out a gleaming stainless-steel cart brimming with food trays. Most patients shuffled toward the dining area, while a few stood aimlessly in the hallway, like Roy.

"Hey, Bono, where's the pleasure?!" exclaimed Roy, although I was only a couple of feet away. He made a move like he was dancing to music.

"Morning, Roy."

"Who's Roy? I'm Beyonce! We should go party, Bono," he said, making a rather obscene pelvic thrust.

"I would, but not now, Beyonce." I made a perfunctory wave with my hand as I entered the nurses' station.

I didn't normally interact with the night nurses, but since I arrived early for my meeting with Shirley Delabrey, I decided to do a quick check-in. Unfortunately, the only nurse on hand was Trina, a forty-something night-shift nurse whose face and body seemed to twitch in tandem when she spoke. She was known by the staff for not making eye contact and overreacting at the slightest implication of wrongdoing, and was secretly nicknamed "Trauma Trina" by the docs. None of the other nurses had these issues, and Trina was written up for complaints several times, from families, patients, and management. I always thought she would do much better as a patient on the unit.

"Morning, Trina. Any news from last night?"

"What do you mean 'news'? Did something happen? I was here the whole time. What? What? What?" she uttered rapid fire, like a machine gun.

"No, no. I mean here on the unit. Any codes? Any changes in behavior?"

"Why do you think we'd have a code? You don't think I can manage these patients? I know what I'm doing. I do. I know. I know."

"Trina," I said, purposely slowing my word flow to a pace that would make most people go insane and want to kill me. "I'm not talking about you, Trina, okay? I just want to know, did anything unusual happen last night? Meds go okay? Everyone eat dinner? I see that Mason's not out here for breakfast."

"Dinner, dinner, dinner, dinner, dinner," she said while scrolling through the notes. "Says here, 'Mason didn't feel like eating.'"

"Just today? Has he been eating breakfast?"

"Jeez, I'm off in five minutes! I'm off. I'm off. I'm off. Sorry, I gotta go." A pronounced twitch undulated throughout her body like a powerful riptide, forcing her knees to partially buckle as she dashed off to the locker room where staff kept their personal belongings.

Since Mason wasn't in the dining area, I decided to stop by his room near the end of the hall. I nodded a "Morning" to JoBee, a mental health tech who was assisting a patient with a walker. A new admit, who I'd never seen, shuffled in my direction. He was holding a towel in his hand. I looked at his nametag and saw his name was Barry.

"Hi, Barry."

"Hey, you got any drugs?" He blankly looked through me.

"Do you mean your medicine?"

"That shit sucks. I want some real drugs, man."

"Tell you what, Barry, I'll check into that for you, okay?"

"Yeah, well I'll stuff this up your ass." He flicked his towel at me like a weapon.

"Did you know the TV's on over there?" I pointed, trying to redirect him.

"Fucking TV. Okay."

I knocked on Mason's door. I heard him answer softly, "Come in." Mason was in bed, lying on his side. His hair was flung haphazardly over his face, and his arms were crossed over his chest. During our brief check-in, he disclosed that the meds weren't changing anything. He still felt listless and lacked an appetite. I explained that we'd meet later that day to explore some thoughts about a new medication that would help him.

"Have you seen those people out there, Doc? Am I really as fucked up as them? Shit. There's a dude out there who thinks I'm Eddie Van Halen."

"That's not so bad. He thinks I'm Bono from U2."

I pulled up a chair and assured him we'd find the right place for him—if not in our clinic then in a more traditional treatment center. In the meantime, I stressed that I didn't want him to skip any meals. When he explained he didn't want to eat with the other patients, I promised to arrange for him to have his meals in his room, at least for now. I looked at my watch, and it was almost 7:30, time to meet his mother. I smiled and said we'd talk later. Mason imperceptibly nodded as I closed his door.

Approaching the nurses' station, I was happy to see Rachelle, a day-shift nurse. I asked her to send meals to Mason's room until further notice, then rushed off for my *sub rosa* appointment.

Shirley Delabrey was already waiting for me. Shirley asked for tea, which I got for her. Then, she took a seat in my office.

"What can I help you with, Shirley?"

"I want to know if you can see me."

"See you? What do you mean?"

"For therapy. Individual therapy."

"Why do you want that?"

"Edward is pressuring me to..."

"To what?"

"Sign the assault complaint. He thinks that if we both do it, then it will stand up better in court."

"I understand your predicament. But it's not for me to tell you what to do. You know that, right?"

"I thought it would help me. You know. Give me strength." Shirley took a deep breath.

I paused, considering the options. I wanted to help this woman, and by helping her to help her son at the same time. What I did next wasn't something I can quite explain. It was very likely unethical, but the words spilled out of my mouth, nonetheless. If my gambit worked, Shirley and her family would be freed from a terribly toxic environment. And so, I said it. Aloud. "Let me ask you something, Shirley. I'd be willing to see you. But only on one condition."

"Condition? What condition?"

"Are you prepared to leave your husband?"

"What?" Her eyes opened wide in an expression of shock.

"I'm sorry, but that's the only way that I would be willing see you. I know it sounds drastic, but it's the only way that I see you making any real progress."

A deep silence pervaded the room. We looked into each other's hearts, making contact in a way that removed all artifice. In that moment I knew the utter fear that gripped her. This was then followed by her abject shame, and my own sense of failure at making her feel this way. I should have known she couldn't leave her gilded prison. Though Edward was the jailer who kept her imprisoned, he was also a safe and known quantity.

Shirley stood, her voice hollow and trembling as she said, "Thank you, anyway, for seeing me."

"Wait. Please." I motioned with an outstretched arm for her to sit back down. "Shirley, I'm sorry if I took you by surprise. Don't you want to talk some more?" But she walked quickly to the door and opened it. There was nothing else I could do but join her. "Don't worry. We'll continue to work together to help Mason. I promise. Thank you, again, for coming in."

As I reached to shake Shirley's hand, she leaned forward and kissed my cheek. I waited at my window until I saw Shirley leave the building. She walked at a brisk pace to the gate. I could not help but wonder what thoughts were running through her mind. All I could think about was how frail and alone she must have felt after our conversation, and how I had taken a major gamble.

And failed miserably.

Over my career, I experienced several patient sessions where I wished I could snap my fingers and have a magical redo. This was one of those times, and I could feel myself falling into a dangerous sinkhole of remorse.

Chapter 9

The morning staff meeting had a certain boring predictability to it. We all sat there, sipping our coffee and shuffling through the papers of dislocated lives, while speaking in a specialized clinical lingo, dissecting diagnoses, prescribing drugs, and choosing treatments and manualized therapies that were often printed out in bulk. I could hardly count how many boxes we clicked each day to satisfy insurance company requirements. How many different digital platforms we used to manage all our records. How distant and mechanical this was from actually working with patients, and yet we devoted a massive amount of our time to doing it.

At some point during the din of discussion, my mind drifted into an odd reverie about whether another kind of healing was possible. I imagined taking a patient's hand and walking with them into their own swampy and dark personal hell. Together, we'd explore, confront, and make sense of the slimy gremlins and frightening swamp creatures, before walking over rough terrain and, exhausted but safe, finding our way back home, to the light. This process would take time, and we would let it unfold naturally, without the pressure of assessments and treatment outcomes. But now, instead of being a healer, had I just become another cog in a massive machine? This was what rattled through my mind when I heard a familiar, though distant voice.

"Ben? Dr. Banks? Ben??"

I looked around with a start. Oh my God! Had I gone into another fit of catalepsy? Did I drool all over my chin? Quickly, I put my hand to my face and stroked my chin as if I were deeply pondering something, when actually I was doing a wet chin check. Nope, that was dry. Did I wet myself? I moved subtly in my chair. No, all seemed dry down there, too. I seemed intact, although my heart pounded like a jackhammer for a couple of beats, and I felt my neck and face flush and tingle.

"Uh, Sorry?" I gulped.

"Well, everyone, I think that's a sign this meeting is going on a bit too long!" Dr. Howell laughed, defusing my embarrassment. "Have you any updates on your cases?"

I pushed some papers around as I shared about the two cases that were close to discharging, and two others that were fairly stable. I didn't divulge any details about my last session with Mason, other than to say that fluoxetine hadn't started working, and that I was considering adding a small, supplemental dose of olanzapine.

The other prescribers in the group shared their mostly positive experiences with that combination for treatment-resistant depression and concurred it was a viable approach. Our gum chewing pharmacist, Mitch, seemed to know the most about it, and he vouched for it.

"Just start him at 5 mils," he nodded knowingly, between chews. "If he responds, bump him to 10."

"Okay, people. That all?" Dr. Beverly started to stand, ready to wrap up the meeting.

"Oh darn! I forgot," I blurted out a little too loudly. Everyone looked at me as I pulled a crinkled packet of papers from my briefcase. "I found this lady who has a therapy animal. She's got her ESA registration. These are her papers. I just thought maybe…"

"Good idea, Ben," responded Beverly enthusiastically. "We've had good results from therapy pets, so let's try her and see if it works out. Okay, everyone, have a good day out there."

Within seconds, everyone had vacated the room. As I packed up my belongings, I reminded Beverly that I was checking with the Chaplain about reserving the chapel for a service for Reggie. She suggested we get a nice flower arrangement, since that was what he loved most.

"Thanks for making this happen." She paused for a long beat. "Tell me, Ben, how about *you*?"

"Huh? I'm sorry about being distracted earlier."

"Holidays can be hard, but *you* know that. If you ever need to talk, about anything…"

"I would, you know. But then you might just have to check me into a room here."

She smiled. "Remember to bring that animal handler in so I can meet her, okay?"

"Will do, Boss," I said, thankful that our conversation ended on a lighter note.

It was drizzling, so I ate my lunch under a covered wooden gazebo on the grounds. Sitting there, I peered out at the street, hoping to see Traveler Jacki and Bear. There was no phone number on her emotional service animal registration form, and I hadn't the faintest idea how to find her. My only hope was to stop by the shelter I recommended to her. If she had stayed there, maybe they could help me locate her. Yes, I'd do that on the way home. Oddly, this small decision gave me a sense of energy and purpose, which surprised me.

Since I was making decisions, I finished eating quickly so I'd have time to stop by the pastoral care office and visit with Chaplain Joyce. I joined her in the chapel, where she was tidying up. When I explained that we wanted to hold a memorial service for Reggie, she was very pleased and fully onboard. She inquired about his religious background, but I couldn't provide anything, other than to say how kind he was.

Joyce raised her hand to make a point. "That reminds me of something the Dalai Lama said."

"Oh? What's that?"

"He said, 'My religion is very simple. My religion is kindness.' Isn't that beautiful? But don't quote me on that." As Joyce chuckled, the delicate laugh lines at the corners of her eyes assembled to enjoy the moment. I couldn't help but notice how her cropped gray hair glowed in soft hues of blue and red from the stained glass in the chapel windows.

We ironed out some of the details, like holding the service on Friday at 12:30 pm, so that staff could attend during lunchtime. Joyce would commence the service, and I'd say a few words, as well as anyone else who wanted to share stories of Reggie. The service would be short, but sweet. Joyce also agreed to arrange with the florist for an arrangement. I left the Chaplain's office feeling uplifted because honoring Reggie's memory felt important to me.

I rushed back to my office, and in the ten minutes before Mason's appointment, I drafted a notice about the memorial and sent it along to Chaplain Joyce. She would finalize it before sending it out to staff. Next, I scanned Mason's previous chart notes. Mostly, I worried how I would respond if there were any new surprises, namely an encounter with his mysterious Traveler or another visit to my home. Just then, there was a faint knock at the door.

I opened the door and invited Mason inside. He appeared lethargic and his affect was still flat, which I documented in my chart notes. He sat in his now familiar posture, legs crossed on the sofa, but with his head hanging down. I started right off with my thoughts on adjusting his medication by adding a small dose of olanzapine, which he readily agreed to.

One of the aspects of Mason's depression I wanted to address was his isolation. And so, I asked him if he had any friends he hung out with in person.

"You mean, not on the computer?"

"Right. *Not* on the computer," I emphasized.

"Nah, not really." His face puckered for a moment, as he thought. "There's this girl who used to visit me. In my room. But my dad and mom stopped that. They were afraid something would happen."

"Afraid of what? What do you mean?"

"They thought we'd mess around."

"Oh. Did you want to?"

"Nah, I just liked Jodi. We went to grammar school and high school together. She graduated with me. We've been buds for years."

"Have you reached out? Let her know what's happening?"

"How? They took away my phone. I can't text her."

"Mason, I was thinking maybe you could do a weekend visit at home soon. Would you be up for that?"

"Yeah? Really? I'd like that."

"That is, if the new medication kicks in and our family work helps. We'll keep an eye on it, okay? In the meantime, your mother can bring in your phone so that you can text Jodi from my office."

Mason swallowed hard. "I don't want her to know."

"And you feel that way because?"

"I'd tell you, but first I'd need that feelings chart you gave me."

I was glad to see Mason felt comfortable enough to kid around with me. It seemed like a good time to talk frankly about the stigma surrounding mental health. We talked about feelings of shame or embarrassment at being in treatment. Eventually, Mason came around and agreed that a real friend, such as Jodi, would understand what he was going through.

We spent the rest of the session exploring his strengths. I had him take a ten-minute online inventory, which revealed his top two strengths as honesty and bravery. Upon learning this, I pointed out that facing fears and getting help was a form of bravery. As an exercise, I told him to put his top strength, honesty, into action once a day, and to track how this affected him and others. I also asked him about any experiences with the Traveler, and was relieved to learn that there had been none.

Before leaving, Mason turned to me and said, "Dr. Banks, I'm sorry you lost your daughter. I'm sure you'll find a way to get through it." I didn't respond, but simply forced a smile. If that was Mason putting his honesty into action, it certainly hit the mark.

Chapter 10

By early the next week, the trajectory of Mason's overall mood was positive. He'd had no more Traveler visits, and he was enjoying his art therapy work. One day, I stopped by the art therapy room to look at the artwork. Art, as it was employed in our unit wasn't meant to treat trauma. It was basically a method for calming and soothing patients. Still, I found the work very expressive. As I looked at the mobiles, clay, and paintings, our art therapist entered. While David prepared materials for an upcoming group, he commented how advanced Mason's work seemed. He said it contained some "powerful imagery."

"What do you mean?" I asked.

David opened a drawer filled with patient self-portraits and pulled out one for me to look at. "Haunting, don't you think?"

In the painting, a fierce, two-headed dragon came out of Mason's abdomen. "Kind of frightening, actually. What do you think it means?" I asked.

"I don't know. Maybe it's a metaphor for a kind of fierce hunger or desire for something?"

I asked David to keep me posted on any other unusual artwork. Later, I added information about the self-portrait to my chart notes. The next day in session, Mason finally shared his art with me—an engraved leather journal he had brought to the hospital with him. But rather than using this as a diary, the blank white pages inside served as sketch pads. The design on the cover resembled something Van Gogh might have conceived. There were birds surrounded by concentric clouds or rings, flying over waves that almost leapt off the page. In the upper right corner was a symbol of the sun, radiating jagged lines of light. It was all carved by hand on thick, ruddy colored leather stock, and the final effect was quite stunning.

When I complimented Mason on his engraving, he broke into a bashful grin. Realizing that he was a visual and tactile learner, I encouraged him to sketch his feelings as a way to get him to express himself. Often, in the hallways, he would sit alone, sketching activity on the unit. Some of these were hilarious caricatures, and I didn't want to know if he'd drawn one of me.

It was midweek, on a bright and cold morning when Shirley came in for a family session. I began by describing to them how family patterns of behavior often spread from one generation to the next, even unconsciously, in what could be imagined as a clan wave. I also noted how Shirley had shown courage and bravery by revealing a hidden history of trauma that was continuing to play itself out in the present moment. I had intentionally chosen to use the word bravery, because I was hoping this might help Mason see how he and his mother both shared the trait.

After letting them both know that the trauma-healing process didn't follow a straight line, I asked if they'd be willing to dialogue about their feelings as a starting point. They agreed, although Mason questioned this approach.

"We never talk together as a family. It's always about accomplishments. Eddie did this or Eddie did that. Dilly did this or Dilly did that. Oh, and Mason's going to talk about his feelings? How does me and my mom talking about feelings change anything? What good is it?"

"Those are interesting thoughts, Mason. The key point here is whenever any single individual in a family makes a change, it's like a ripple that moves outward and changes the entire system. If I touch my fingertip into a cup of water, what happens? It generates a ripple that moves through the entire cup, right? But you're right in that we don't need to talk about feelings, per se. Any new understanding we have has the power to change a family, even a little bit at a time."

I decided to use an Internal Family Systems technique with Mason and Shirley. As I explained to them, Internal Family Systems, or IFS, was a healing modality designed to help anyone connect with the various sub-personalities, or parts of themselves. "Yes, we have a core self, but then there's the anxious self, the confident self, the sad self, the wounded self, the artistic self, the wise self and so on. You can even contact any part of you that helped endure and overcome abuse."

"The wise-ass self?" Mason mischievously lifted his eyebrows.

"Oh. I think you've already gotten in touch with that self," I winked. Finally, I emphasized that they were to bring a sense of openness and curiosity to the task. And, if they had any problem communicating with a part, they could always ask for permission to do so. If any part was hurting, then that could be addressed as well. We went through the introductory process slowly, and by the end of the session, both Mason and his mother seemed more willing to explore their "parts."

Even though we just scratched the surface, each was able to identify one or two parts of themselves that were helpful in their own healing. For example, Shirley pinpointed her "nurturing" part while Mason identified his "angry self" part. At least it was a start, and it offered them a way of watching and listening to their "parts" or inner workings, as an outside observer might—from a more detached and safer place. "Just remember," I affirmed, "old hurts and trauma can be healed, and you started that process today. But it takes time. You tapped into your inner resources, and you were both very brave. And honest."

I could feel the burst of positive energy between Shirley and Mason. It was a constructive emotional experience for both of them to be vulnerable and to be heard. Just before our time was up, I reiterated the progress Mason made over the past two weeks. Then, I floated the idea of Mason getting a weekend pass to spend a bit of time at home.

Mason perked up. "When?"

"Maybe this week, or the week after? And maybe Mason could invite one of his friends over for dinner?" I looked at Shirley, who demurred for a moment as I held my breath.

"Sure, why not? That would be delightful." She nudged Mason with her elbow.

"And, Mason, remember what we talked about? You need to contact your friend."

"Mom, my phone?"

Shirley fished a phone out of her rather large purse and handed it to Mason, who started a flurry of texting. "Does this mean I can get out of here soon?" asked Mason. His eyes were glued to his phone as it pinged with an incoming text.

"When that time comes, you'll be the first to know. But a weekend pass is a good first step. There's still a lot of work I want us to do. And when you are ready, I want to transition you to an outpatient therapist. Plus, there's the question of where's the best place for you to live, and finding goals for working or education."

"Oh." Mason scrunched his face in a way that told me he was not so happy with my extended answer.

As they walked away, Mason was still texting. It felt good to know that there was a glimmer of hope for them. It was only a few minutes later, while writing up my chart notes, that there was a knock at the door. I wasn't expecting anyone and was surprised to see that Shirley had returned.

"Did you forget something?" I looked around the office for an errant hat or purse.

"No. I wanted to wait until Mason was gone."

"What is it, Shirley?"

"You know that complaint Edward wanted me to sign? I just wanted to let you know. I didn't sign it."

"I see."

"I'm praying it will work out."

"Me too. Is that it?"

"Yes. Yes."

"Good. Thank you for letting me know." It was the first time Shirley appeared hopeful, and it made me smile.

"You're an angel for helping my son. And me."

Despite this good news, I had a bad feeling of what was coming next, so I quickly clasped my hands behind my back and did a back-leaning limbo move. It was my personal, all-time best therapist move for avoiding physical contact with patients. It rarely failed, so I was chagrined when Shirley moved in with Samurai-like swiftness and kissed me hard, leaving her lavender lip mark on my cheek. Nonetheless, I was pleased that she had refused to give in to her husband's demands. But as with all my patients, I knew there would be some hairpin curves to navigate up ahead.

Chapter 11

I stayed at the clinic late on Wednesday after co-facilitating the last DBT group of the day with Sarah. It was my turn to chart, which was fairly easy since we only had five of the highest functioning patients in the group. I wasn't sure how many of them grasped the ideas of interpersonal effectiveness and behavioral sequences, but I knew Mason had. He had asked questions about dealing with someone who was "domineering." Did he want to use interpersonal skills to modify his own behavior toward his father? It seemed so, and I wrote a note to remind myself to ask him about this. In any event, his thinking patterns and mood convinced me to give him that weekend pass. I also noticed he was interacting well with the other patients. He was even eating meals in the group dining room.

After charting, I caught up on several new journals that crammed my inbox. My reading this evening included the journal *Science*, my subscription to *Journal Watch Depression/Anxiety*, and the ever scintillating *American Psychosomatic Society*. For example, did you know that patients with HIV had a greater risk for depression, which in turn made those patients more at risk for cardiovascular disease? I'm not sure how all these studies were helpful, but at least I felt more like a professional for having read them.

It was completely dark out when I was finished. Jeff, the security guard, stood upright inside the front entrance, arms firmly crossed around his chest. "'Night, Doc Ben," he said, giving me a perfunctory nod. When I reached the creaky front gate, I turned back to look at the hospital. From November through the winter, additional floodlights were turned on to brighten up the building and the grounds. But instead of softening the brick building's few Gothic-inspired features, it seemed to accentuate them. Especially those tall, almost spooky looking spires. But what I saw illuminated almost caused me to drop my briefcase.

I clearly saw a large figure on the roof! It was situated on an extremely steep area, just beneath the Chapel spire. Was it an animal? I ran up to get a better look and stood where one of the floodlights beamed on that section of roof. From my vantage point, there was no doubt it was definitely a person. He was sitting there, legs crossed, as if meditating. I had an immediate sense of having seen that sitting figure before, in my office. When a strong gust of wind blew the long black hair from the face, it revealed distinctive features I knew well.

It was Mason. He had a supremely serene expression on his face. I'd never seen him look so calm and composed, and perhaps that's what worried me the most. What was he planning on doing from his dangerously high perch?

I was stunned and immobile for a moment while deciding what to do. I didn't want to frighten him, but I didn't want him doing anything rash, either. So I did what any trained professional would do. I shouted at the top of my lungs, "Mason, don't move! Do you hear me? Don't move!!" I repeated this several times more, but Mason was unflappable, placidly sitting there without a worry in the world. He almost seemed to have a smile on his lips.

I wasn't sure he needed any help, but I cried out anyway, "Mason! Don't worry, it will be okay! Stay right there and we'll come get you!"

I ran back inside and picked up the phone. I must have looked quite alarmed because Jeff pulled a concealed Glock pistol from under his jacket. Then, he deftly pulled back the gun's slide, which put a round in the chamber. He had proudly shown this action to me before, but it didn't comfort me now.

"What's wrong, Doc Ben? Should I lock the unit down?"

"No. We've got an elopement, not a code. So Jeff, please take that round out of the chamber." I jabbed my fingers at the phone to access the intercom. "This is Dr. Banks. We have an elopement from the Psych Unit. Please check all doors and do a patient count."

"Doc Ben, who got out?"

"Where are the access doors to the roof? We need to get up there. Now!"

"Sure, there's one I know of. A ladder inside the utility room," replied Jeff as we entered the unit. The utility room was dirty and musty, and we found the ladder. Jeff went first, and he pushed a large panel open and grunted his way through the opening and onto the roof. When I got to the top, he gave me a hand and hoisted me through. I tried to get my bearings and locate the Chapel.

"He was just below the Chapel spire, looking out toward the front of the building."

"This way. Follow me, Doc." As we crouched along, Jeff held onto a low-slung railing that ran around the perimeter. "Is he violent?"

"No, no. Absolutely not! Let me approach him. Please just stay in the background. No guns. I'm sure I can get him to cooperate."

"Whatever you say."

The shingles were dangerously slippery where moss had

formed. Finally, we clambered to the portion of the roof where I'd seen Mason. "What the... where in the..." I stammered.

"Do you think he jumped?"

"Oh my God, I hope not." Suddenly, though, I wondered if that was a possibility. "Let's circumnavigate the roof, you go in one direction I'll go in the other. That way if he's still up here one of us will see him."

"Gotcha." Jeff headed off in one direction; I took off in the other. By the time we met back up, I was exhausted, my hands, ankles, and legs aching from walking at such a steep angle.

"Spot him?"

"No," I huffed, trying to catch my breath.

"Could be a jumper."

"Jeff, you're just trying to make my day, huh?"

"Sorry, Doc. Just sayin'."

"If we can't find him, we'll have to call the police." I closed the roof panel before climbing back down the ladder.

Immediately, I went to the nurses' station to ask about Mason eloping. Certainly, someone there would have seen him leave the unit. The night nurse, Nancy, confirmed that all the patients were accounted for and had gone to bed.

"He's in his room. Sleeping." Nancy switched on the video showing Mason's room. For patient protection, each room had closed circuit video. Despite seeing what looked like someone asleep in Mason's room, I marched down the hall with Jeff and Nancy in tow. I knocked lightly before entering and switching on the light.

Mason squinted at us, looking confused. "Huh, what's happening?"

"Nothing, Mason. Sorry. Go back to bed."

I was still convinced that Mason had somehow escaped notice. After canceling the elopement call, I insisted that we watch the entire recorded video from the time Mason entered his room for sleep to when Jeff and I were on the rooftop. The video proved Mason never left his room and was soundly asleep the entire time.

"So tell me again, Doc. What was it you saw out there?"

"Well, it was dark, Jeff. Very dark."

"A squirrel? They can get pretty big, you know."

"Yeah, a squirrel." I grabbed my briefcase and left the unit as fast as I could. I thought I heard snickering as I exited, but I couldn't be sure.

Outside, I paced every inch of the grounds. I couldn't find a carcass or an animal anywhere. What the hell was that I saw? If it wasn't Mason, what was it? Even though I was unsettled by what had happened—or didn't happen?—I decided to check out the shelter where I hoped to locate Traveler Jacki and Bear.

It was past eight o'clock, and it occurred to me that I hadn't let Beth know of my whereabouts. There was a time when I'd text or call even if I was going to be just a few minutes late. Now, the chasm between us was so large that I rarely let her know. I wondered if she would even notice?

When I reached 26th street, I turned left and slowed down. The neighborhood was bleak and barren. Several store fronts were boarded up, and huddled shapes dotted the sidewalks. I wondered if I'd made a mistake by sending Traveler Jacki out this way.

Just then, I saw it. A neon Rose City Shelter sign flickered, threatening to burn out at any second. I easily found a parking spot and walked past two heavily stubbled men who were drinking beer from cans and loitering near the entrance. The lighting inside was dim, but I could make out a hodgepodge of worn chairs and tables. At the front desk of what must have been a hotel at some point in time, I greeted a short woman wearing a white and red bandana over her hair. She looked up from a yellowed ledger and set down her pen.

"What can I do ya'?" She looked me up and down, her deep-set brown eyes narrowing.

"I'm looking to find a woman."

"Ain't we all," she retorted.

"No, no. You see, it's someone I know. Well actually, I just met her a couple of times. By chance. It's not what you think. She had this little dog, and I thought maybe she stayed here. About five feet five. Not the dog," I stammered, with a nervous smile. The woman didn't blink an eye.

"Got a white feather in her hair?"

"Yes. Yes! A white feather, that's her. Is she here? Do you know where…"

"Stayed one night. Ain't seen her since. No clue where she went."

I paused, looking around at people whose lives, for whatever reason, had taken an uncertain turn. I felt like I needed to be here a little longer. "Do you mind if I, uhm, have a seat. Sit down for a bit?"

"Knock yourself out," she said, returning to write in her ledger.

And so, I sat at on a rickety bamboo chair that sagged and crackled under my weight. A lanky man with thinning brownish-gray hair, probably in his fifties, came and sat on a chair adjacent to mine. He was shivering, coughing intermittently, and wearing a threadbare jacket that was at least one size too small. He kept tugging on the jacket, vainly trying to cover his chest. We had a short conversation about nothing in particular. The weather, the local sports team. And yet, there was something comforting here, a sense of belonging, if even for a brief moment. When I stood up to go, I reached into my pockets and fetched my leather gloves.

"Here. These help?"

"Nah, I couldn't."

"Please…" He reached out, tried them on. Then, with his gloves on, he pulled his jacket tight, with his hands resting on his chest. He was still sitting there like that when I glanced back.

By the time I got home it was after 10:00 pm. The TV was off and Beth was not in the living room. I figured she must have gone to bed. I wanted to go into Mel's room, but for the first time in almost a year, I chose not to. I wanted desperately to talk with Beth, but knew that was out of the question.

Lying in bed, I felt disloyal for not stopping in Mel's room. I knew that didn't make sense, but a restlessness was brewing in me, and I couldn't put my finger on it, except to know it was profoundly disturbing and disquieting. I was certain of only one thing. Mason's eerie appearance on the roof had me questioning the very foundation of my own reality and sanity.

Chapter 12

The next morning as I walked up the path to the hospital entrance, I couldn't take my eyes off the rooftop. Worse, I knew I'd have to account for what had happened the previous night. And I was right.

The moment I walked into the staff room, Dr. Rick greeted me while trying to stifle a smirk. Unsuccessfully, I might add. My faux pas was called out at the top of the meeting.

Beverly spoke right up. "The night nurse documented a safety event. Ben, what can you tell us about that? You thought we had an elopement?"

"First of all, aren't safety events for patient safety? I don't understand why this was even written up."

"Well, you were climbing on the roof at night with security officer Jeff, correct? I'd say that merits safety event status."

"Sorry, but I still don't see how it was a *patient* safety event."

"Ben, I understand your point. But it involves safety in the sense it disrupted the staff. Several patients were awakened and disoriented when doing the count. One slipped and fell, so that's your safety event right there that needs to be written up. Are we happy now?"

"Okay, well, I didn't know that."

"I think it might help if you could tell us what happened from your point of view." Beverly stared at me with a steely expression.

"Squirrel," muttered Rick to pharmacist Mitch who was sitting beside him. I shot Rick a look, and he turned his gaze away from me.

"Honestly, Beverly, I don't know what it was. From a distance, it looked like a person. Then when I got closer, I thought it was Mason."

Beverly raised her hands over her mouth for a moment. She remained like this, pondering for a few seconds before lowering her hands. "Ben, I'm concerned you're getting too close to this patient."

"No, this... this isn't about that. It was dark. Really dark, so..."

"Have you considered countertransference? You have some very strong feelings about this case."

"But I literally saw something up there. That's not countertransference. I mean, it could have been a big squirrel or other animal. Even Jeff said so."

"So maybe, in the future, let's get confirmation first from another staff member the next time something like this happens, okay?"

It wasn't the kind of support I'd hoped for. But given the circumstances, it was probably more than I deserved. The rest of the meeting was without incident and as boring as usual. At the very least, I thought, I'd managed to inject some excitement into everyone's water cooler banter.

Later that morning, however, Beverly made a surprise visit to my office. She had access to my digital schedule, and she conveniently knocked on my door during a half-hour period where I was free.

"Mind if I come in?"

"Sure. Have a seat."

"That's okay, Ben. This won't take long." She entered and closed the door behind her. "I just wanted to see how you're doing. Everything okay?"

"Beverly, I understand that whole thing yesterday was out of the ordinary, but…"

"Look, Ben, I'm not blaming you for anything. But I need to know if you've been experiencing any neurologic issues."

"Huh? Neurologic?"

"Headaches, problems with cognition, vision, forgetfulness?"

"No, absolutely not."

"Have you been drinking or using any…"

"Hell no. Well, not at work, anyway. Sure, I have a glass of wine after… Why are you asking me this?"

"As Executive Director, I'm responsible for your work, you know that, right? It's my job to minimize risk and keep everything in ship-shape order."

I took a deep breath and felt a wave of tension release. "Okay. You're right, Beverly. I understand."

"Maybe we should transfer Mason to another therapist?"

"Please don't. Truth is, I was really embarrassed by what happened. I can't explain it, either, which concerns me. But if you transferred him, that would look like I couldn't do my job."

"Okay. He's your patient. *For now.* And if it's any consolation, word on the street is we have some pretty gnarly squirrels around here." We shared a laugh, and she gave me a quick hug before leaving. I would have promised to let her know if anything was up with me, but I didn't want to make promises I couldn't keep.

For the rest of the day, stealing a free minute here and there, I worked on my eulogy for Reggie, wondering how best to honor him. Finally, I realized that the best way to commemorate him was by sharing our conversations, and letting him speak in his own words. While this lifted my spirits, my mind kept ruminating on my upcoming session with Mason. That time came soon enough.

Mason situated himself on the red couch in his favorite position, legs crossed, Buddha style. Or, should I say, roof style? We exchanged pleasantries, and he said he was feeling as good as he had all week. The new medication was working.

As written in my chart notes:

The patient's affect was positive and upbeat. Patient reports that the addition of olanzapine 5 mg, has helped him feel more energetic, and he reports asking for permission to walk briskly through the halls for exercise, and says, "It felt really good to move around. I'd like to do more of that once I go outside."

Mason had assiduously followed up on the assignment I'd given him of sharing his strength of honesty one time a day. He reported that he did this by telling others how they were being helpful, or by honestly examining his own thoughts and behavior. For the next week, I gave him a brand-new assignment. This time, he was to engage his strength of bravery once a day. He was to keep a journal of his experiences—in his case a sketch journal that depicted how bravery made a difference. Studies had shown that this simple exercise was an effective tool for reducing depression and upregulating positive affect. I was glad to see it was already making an impact for Mason.

Delicately, I broached the subject of Mason's future, of looking at how he could move forward in a constructive way— either through learning or vocational training of some kind. The elephant in the room, of course, was that his father didn't want him living in the house. And, to be fair, neither did Mason really want to reside there. After querying him, however, it was obvious Mason didn't have the foggiest idea of what he might do in terms of a livelihood.

"If you don't have a path, how can you be independent?" I

asked him.

"Don't know," he mumbled at the floor.

"This might be kind of branching off from what we've been working on, but I think it could help you." I remembered a brief career quiz that he could explore. When I mentioned this, he seemed interested enough to take a fifteen-minute online career quiz in my office. The analysis showed he liked to work alone, and that he was creative and liked design. By the end of our time, Mason at least understood that there were pathways for someone with his creative skill set and sensibilities.

"Thanks, Dr. Banks." Mason started to stand.

"Not so fast."

"I thought it was time." He pointed at the clock beside him.

"Mason, something happened last night."

"Last night?" he repeated, his lips stitched tightly while glancing sideways.

"Right, last night."

"I don't know what you mean."

"You saw the Traveler didn't you?" There was a long silence. "Tell me the truth, Mason."

"I thought if I told you, you wouldn't let me go home this weekend."

"No, you can still visit home."

"I can? Really?"

"Yep, we'll get it set up." Mason brushed the hair off his forehead and flashed a brief smile. "So, are you going to tell me?"

"Uhm, last night I was feeling kind of bad. I kept thinking, 'Am I ever going to get out of here?' Anyway, I lied down and not long after, I saw the Traveler. He stepped out of the dark and whispered to me, 'You are not a prisoner.' Next thing I know, he guided me onto the rooftop. So I figured I'd stay up there."

"People-can't-leave-their-body," I said. My speech grew stilted and wooden, as if the words could not be contained in a single sentence.

"It was so peaceful... with the stars and the wind. A big white owl flew down and sat with me for a while."

"People-can't-be-in-two-places-at-once. It was an illusion, a mental projection of some kind."

"But I heard you calling me, telling me not to move or do anything."

"No, you didn't!" I shouted out of frustration, before catching myself and taking a breath. "Look, we'll figure it out. Things like this just don't happen, okay?" Mason glowered at me as I went to the couch and sat next to him. I took a deep breath before saying, "I'm really sorry. I'm just having a hard time understanding. Please forgive me."

"Okay, can I go now?" I nodded and Mason stood up.

"Mason, wait," I said plaintively as he paused by the door. "I just want you to know, it hurts me very much to think I've disappointed you. This is my own failing, not yours. I'm the fuck-up here, and..."

Mason let go a sigh as his shoulders relaxed. "Thanks, Doc. No worries. And you're not a fuck-up. I should know."

"Maybe..." We looked at one another in silence for what seemed like a minute until we both smiled. That smile turned into an unexpected eruption of shared laughter. Finally, after the laughter died down, I gave Mason a hug, which he returned. I knew that having physical contact with patients was frowned upon nowadays, but it wasn't always like this. Besides, the authentic feelings I shared, the laughter and the hug were probably better than any other therapy I could have formulated for the situation.

"I'm going to call your mother right now to give her the good news, okay?" As he walked down the hall, Mason had more bounce in his step. Moments later, I called Shirley and explained the plan was for her to pick up her son tomorrow at the end of the day and bring him back on Sunday evening.

While I was happy for Mason and his mother, I was personally glad to get a break, however brief, from all the strange and bizarre happenings swirling around Mason. I had always loved my work, but now I was almost dreading coming in to the office. It felt like the clinic was a pot and somehow, I was a lobster being slow-cooked.

Still, I felt horrible having raised my voice at Mason. How could I have been so callous as to diminish another's experience? Just then I became aware of a pounding behind my eyes and the back of my head. I massaged my temples, hoping this tension wouldn't turn into a full-blown migraine. I noticed my vision seemed blurry. "Jeez," I thought, rolling my eyes up in pain. "Could this be neurologic like Beverly mentioned?"

I had always told patients that stress in the body was a warning signal letting them know something in their life was out of balance and needed changing. Was I getting such a message? That's when the unthinkable popped into my head.

Am I having a psychotic break?

No, I quickly reassured myself. The idea that I was having a psychotic break was just my medical training talking. Still, it became clear to me that somehow, I needed to power wash this so-called Traveler business from my mind. That's when, thankfully, I remembered Katerina, a former, trusted supervisor. If anyone could help me, it would be her. Through a clenched jaw and throbbing head, I left this message on her voicemail:

Hi, Katerina, it's Ben here. Hope you're doing well. I'm calling because I want to set up a visit with you. So the sooner the better, even this weekend. I need your help right away. Much love. Bye.

Then, I sat in my chair and closed my eyes for a few minutes. I tried to breathe and empty my mind like I'd learned in a meditation class. I don't know if my mind emptied, but after a short while the tension lessened, and somehow, I got through the rest of the day.

Later that evening, I was still feeling guilty about not visiting the Shrine of Mel. So I stopped in for a few moments.

"Hi, Mel, sorry I didn't visit yesterday." I sat on the bed and imagined that she was responding. "What's that you say? You were busy anyhow? Okay, well, that's good then." Then, I hung out in the Shrine of Mel for about half an hour, feeling better and pondering what Mel would have thought about the Traveler.

Chapter 13

On the drive to work, there was one constant word that I couldn't seem to banish from my head.

Loss.

What was it about the losses that were piling up all around me? It wasn't just Mel, but Reggie dying alone, that poor bastard Sasquatch stuck there in the forensic unit, and those lost souls at the Rose City Shelter, sucking down one last brew or chucking up their lungs because of TB or who knows what? And also my patients, most of whom had moved on, but to where? Even Mason, despite all of my efforts, would very likely end up adrift, without a home, given the rigidity and intractability of his father.

I could feel myself tensing up, so I did what I instructed anxious patients to do. I relaxed my body, took a couple of deep breaths, holding each for the count of four, before exhaling slowly. It worked great, until I realized that Reggie's memorial service was today, and I still wasn't a hundred percent sure of what I was going to say. Yes, I convinced myself, that's what was stirring my existential pot!

It was okay, I told myself, positive that this must be the wise and supportive part of me telling the anxious and insecure part of me to calm the fuck down. Simply recognizing my *parts*, as I often guided patients to do, made me laugh aloud.

Yes, it would be okay. I was going to be okay.

The email for Reggie's memorial had been sent out, and Chaplain Joyce announced it over the PA system more than once. I printed out a couple of pages of my own recollections about Reggie and stuffed them inside my coat pocket. When I arrived at the chapel, the turnout exceeded my expectation. There were at least thirty people seated, with a few more coming in. There were people from other units, occupational therapists, social workers, nurses and mental health techs whom I'd never met. It was obvious that Reggie had touched many people during his stay here.

The flower arrangement was positioned beside the podium. It was filled with red, orange and yellow blossoms, containing dahlias, ornamental grasses, camellias and more. There were even appetizing seasonal red apples and green pears on the table. Reg would have loved that, I thought, as Chaplain Joyce approached.

"How's this?" she asked, nodding at the floral arrangement.

"Beautiful. Thanks for setting that up, Joyce."

"Should we get started, then?"

I nodded and sat down in the front. Joyce dimmed the lights, which accentuated the natural light flooding in from the stained glass windows. Joyce walked to the front of the podium and the room quieted to a hush. Joyce paused, then spoke about relationships being the most important thing in life. She touched on Reggie's length of stay at the hospital, and how he had shared his deep sense of devotion, service to others and joy with all of us. It was a moving and touching testament to Reggie, and as I took out my notes, I hoped I could be half as inspiring.

At the podium, I paused for a beat to look out at the audience and give them a moment to settle. That's when I noticed a woman waving at me from the back of the room. A long white feather loping alongside her head caught my eye. This momentarily threw me, until I realized, "Of course, Traveler Jacki's here! She's so strange that it makes perfect, if illogical, sense." A smile crept across my lips as I gave her a nod of recognition.

Then, I took a nervous breath and uncomfortably looked at my notes. I made a few halting, disconnected statements, before saying, "You know, on second thought, I think I better put down these notes. I never saw Reggie take notes on anything, and he would definitely not approve." Uncharacteristically, I ripped my notes in half, producing a short burst of laughter. I told how Reggie treated his plants like each was special. In fact, he possessed an almost magical sense of knowing what each one needed. Once, when I asked him how he did this, he said, "It's easy. You just listen. If you get really quiet and listen to anyone or anything with love, they'll share with you all their secrets." And that, I concluded, was Reggie's all-natural, organic ingredient for happiness.

When I was done, no one stood except Beverly. I stepped down and walked toward the back of the room. I couldn't see what was happening, but only heard a gasping shriek from the crowd of mourners. I spun around to see my worst nightmare. It was Sasquatch. He must have entered from a side door near where Beverly was walking. He had one meat-sized hand clamped around Beverly's waist. In his other hand was a large carving knife, which he held up to her neck.

"It's okay, it's okay, everyone back away," said Beverly, breathless.

I looked around for a phone and saw one on the wall near me. I dialed into the intercom system as fast as I could. "Code Silver in the Chapel! Code Silver!"

Sasquatch was ranting and muttering, "Kill the shark, the shark is here, I see you shark."

I opened the double back doors. "Everyone leave this room. Now," I ordered in a loud but composed voice. The fewer people around, the less chance there was of Sasquatch harming anyone. And, I felt that Sasquatch would be easier to handle without interference and confusion. I noticed that Chaplain Joyce was helping guide people back into the hall.

Two of our largest orderlies, Burt and Fredo, sprinted into the room. They were each gripping IMs, intramuscular syringes loaded with Haldol, our go-to emergency tranquilizer for agitation and aggressive behavior. But when they saw Sasquatch, whose face contorted and eyes darted wildly back and forth, swinging the knife at an imaginary shark, or God knows what, they stopped in their tracks and gawked at one another.

"Here's the plan," I said to them. "I'll go first, you two follow me. We'll come up from behind. I'll get his attention and try to quiet him. When I give the signal, you give the IM. Then use whatever restraint is necessary. Okay?"

That's about the time when our security guard, Danny, showed up. He'd assessed the situation, his gun already drawn. "Danny, no, no, no." I tugged his arm down. "Put that away. No one is going to get shot here. We have a plan."

Amid the chaos, I heard the incongruous sound of a dog barking and growling. We all turned to see a small black and white spaniel turned attack dog. It grabbed and snapped at Sasquatch's ankles, causing him to hop and shake his legs.

Thinking the dog might actually distract the big man, I quickly motioned for Burt and Fredo to follow me. Sasquatch took a couple of wild swings at the dog with his knife, but missed. We were getting closer when I heard the rhythmic sound of a beating drum, along with someone singing. "Oh shit," I grumbled under my breath, not believing my eyes.

It was Traveler Jacki. She was loudly beating a hand drum, all the while dancing in a snake-like fashion right toward Sasquatch. Frantically, I motioned for her to back off, but she didn't respond. Her voice was low and the syllables both halting and long. I couldn't make out any words, but the effect was captivating, reminding me of the Native American rituals I had seen.

She was within arms' reach of Sasquatch when her singing and beating reached a crescendo. At that moment, Sasquatch released his grip on Beverly, who slipped beneath and out of his reach. Watching the big man's body movements, I noticed his eyes had stopped jerking side to side. His arm holding the knife seemed to relax and lower slightly. Seeing this shift, I hoisted my hand, signaling for Burt and Fredo to pause. Beverly joined us, and we all watched in amazement at what was unfolding.

The volume and rhythm of Traveler Jacki's song and drum softened. She must have made some kind of nonverbal contact with Bear, who immediately stopped growling and biting at Sasquatch's ankles. The dog actually started to sing, as well as spaniels can sing, along with Traveler Jacki. Together they simultaneously crooned, snake-danced, and circled Sasquatch several times as his eyes grew heavily lidded.

Sasquatch's head began to totter as the drumming and singing grew softer and softer until finally, Traveler Jacki was close enough to gently take the knife from the big man's hand. Setting the knife down on the ground, she took Sasquatch by the hand and guided him to the altar, where they both sat down.

Bear leaped into Sasquatch's lap and contentedly laid down ready for a nap. Sasquatch also seemed ready for a nap as he gently petted the little dog's head.

Traveler Jacki looked over to me and motioned that I could approach and take Sasquatch. Along with the orderlies, we tiptoed closer. Sasquatch didn't flinch in the slightest at our presence. Burt stood, poised with his syringe, waiting for a signal. When I whispered "okay," he injected the IM without getting any resistance.

"Better put him in the seclusion room." I knew that Sasquatch would be monitored, observed through the door, and documented on as according to state law. We'd have to notify his mother as well, but that would be the task of the forensic doctors and staff.

"For sure, do it," confirmed Beverly, who was visibly shaking. I put my arm over her shoulders as Burt and Fredo, shadowed by our guard, Danny, escorted Sasquatch out of the Chapel and into seclusion.

"Oh my goodness." Beverly turned to Traveler Jacki and grabbed her hand. "First of all, thank you. And secondly, *who* in the world are you?"

"This is the new pet handler and her emotional service animal I told you about," I said to Beverly. "You said we could give them a try out?"

"That was one hell of a try out for me, honey. You've got the job!"

This Code Silver was quite the jolt of adrenaline for everyone, and I promised Beverly I'd make a follow-up announcement for staff as soon as I was sure Sasquatch was safely in seclusion.

Before departing, Beverly tugged on my arm. "Ben, could you join me for lunch today?"

"Sure. Depends on the time."

"Say, thirty minutes?"

I glanced at my phone calendar. "I have a two o'clock, so that should give me time to tie up the loose ends here and meet you at the cafeteria."

"Good, see you there."

Traveler Jacki was helping the Chaplain put away some folding chairs and clean up the Chapel. I approached and asked Traveler Jacki if she could meet me later, about 4:00 pm to set up the therapy animal schedule. She agreed, and I rushed off to the forensic unit.

Sasquatch appeared heavily sedated, and was under observation by Dr. Robert Trent. I knew Bob well, back from my days working forensics. He had the kind of easy going and unflappable demeaner which I admired.

"Hey, Bob. How's he doing?"

"Not bad, Ben. See for yourself." Bob moved aside so I could look through the unbreakable glass window. "He's stable now, but I heard he gave you quite a scare."

"No shit. He got into the cafeteria and found a knife."

"That's his signature weapon of choice, you know."

"I know. How long will you hold him here?"

"I see no reason to keep him more than an hour or two if he remains quiet."

"I wonder what set him off. I'm thinking maybe a med-related issue?"

"Very good, Sherlock. The new on-call nurse missed his morning dose."

It was from forensics that I made an announcement over the intercom letting all the staff know the Code Silver was no longer in effect and everyone was safe. Lastly, I added, "Thanks to all who attended Reggie's memorial. It was certainly one for the ages. We'll always remember you, Reggie."

Chapter 14

Beverly sat alone at a table in a far corner of the cafeteria. After setting my tray down and joining her, she thanked me for the message that I'd delivered to the staff.

"I found out why Sasquatch had a psychotic episode." I then explained that he had missed his meds because of a miscommunication between the night and day nursing shifts. "I don't mean to throw anyone under the bus, but this will need to be in the police report."

"You're right, Ben. That's normal procedure when there's a threat. But since no one was injured, I'd rather there be no public knowledge of this. And we can tell the Joint Commission when the time is more right."

"Is there a reason to be concerned about the Joint Commission?"

"No, not at all. Only..." Beverly covertly glanced around the room. "There's going to be a big announcement very soon."

"Announcement? About what?"

"That's what I wanted to talk with you about," she said, leaning forward in her chair. "You can't tell anyone, Ben. It's a major hospital expansion. We have a lot of land out front that we can build on. Picture if you can, an expansive glass entryway fronted by a dramatic bronze sculpture or two. It'll modernize the entire image of the hospital and make us more of a regional center. And," she paused, lowering her voice, "there's a very good chance we'll need a new Executive Director. Someone with vision who wants to make a real difference. Maybe someone sitting at this table?"

I was nonplussed and afraid that my jaw dropped by at least an inch. Beverly seemed not to notice. But I couldn't quite understand why she would offer me such a plumb position. "Beverly, if you don't mind my asking. Why me?"

"Ben, this should come as no surprise. Everyone here can see you're experiencing burnout. It happens to everyone. It happened to me before I became an Executive Director. I think you need another professional challenge. Are you up for it?"

Yes, burnout and compassion fatigue would explain my reaction to a lot of things that were happening in my life. I'd lost my resilience. Maybe she was right about making a change. "I'd definitely consider it, Beverly. Strongly consider it."

"Excellent, good to hear."

"But what about you?"

Beverly smiled confidently, speaking with obvious excitement. "I'm the one who created this plan and came up with the funding. For that, I hope to serve on the Board of Directors. I want us to be a regional force, and there are other hospitals we can purchase." She took a breath, bringing her voice down to a hush-hush level. "We're so close, Ben. We can't afford the slightest little glitch. If news about the assault got out, well, you understand. That's why I was hoping you'd do the report without any police involvement. What do you say?"

"I'd want to include recommendations for making sure this couldn't happen again."

"Absolutely. I can't wait to see your recommendations."

I couldn't suppress a grin. "So, uhm, when did you say you

wanted that report?"

After lunch, I felt uplifted and revitalized, like I was walking on air. For quite some time I had been feeling like I was in a rut with my direct patient care. The idea of being an Executive Director was professionally invigorating and got me excited. I imagined shaping an entire hospital where trauma-informed care was truly practiced and informed by humane and integrative healing modalities. For the first time in a while, I envisioned the hospital through the eyes of a prospective Executive Director.

My investigation proceeded immediately, and it involved interviewing the forensics unit and all the staff and persons involved in what happened before, during and after the event. As it turned out, there was no mystery to Sasquatch's elopement. He had simply followed behind one of the mental health techs who punched in the door code and pushed the food cart out of the unit. From the hallway, Sasquatch could have easily entered the kitchen and found a stray knife.

My investigation included interviewing Traveler Jacki, who was waiting for me in the lobby at 4:00 pm just as I'd asked. I escorted her and Bear to my office where I entered Jacki's information in our computer system. As I suspected, though, there was a small problem with her address. She didn't have one.

"Jacki, I need to input an address for you."

"Just put down this address. I'll be around here anyways."

"Maybe I can say you're transitioning," I thought, finding an empty computer field to make an entry.

"Transitioning. That's a fancy word for being a Traveler, ain't it, Bear?" She rubbed Bear under his chin as he appeared to smile.

"Okay. What about your social?"

"My what?"

"Your Social Security number."

"Is that important?"

"You have one, don't you?"

"Probably, but I ain't so good with numbers. 'Sides, this is a volunteer position, and you ain't paying me so..."

"Sorry, Traveler Jacki, but we need that card because you get meal vouchers. I'm guessing you want the meals."

"Ohhh, it's the *card* you want? I got one of those." Jacki dug into her backpack quickly producing a Social Security card that looked like it came fresh off the printing press. "Here it is!"

"This looks brand new. Where'd you get this?" I was shocked to see such a pristine, laminated card when everything else in her backpack looked like it was years old.

"It is new. Uhm, I got the old one replaced the other day."

"Where at? Where'd you go?" I doubted she could come up with a reasonable answer.

"That place. You know, the Social Security card store."

It was all too incredulous, but since she saved our Executive Director from a psychotic madman and made me look good, I decided not to pursue any follow-up questions. Besides, I was pretty sure many street people lived off the grid without ever using their Social Security numbers.

After entering Jacki in the computer system, we created a workable therapy animal schedule. She was especially interested in learning about the kinds of patients who lived on the unit. Without breaching confidentiality, I shared some of the patient's favorite things, such as how Roy liked music, Wanda liked coffee, and Mason liked art. Finally, I explained that I was writing a report of the events earlier that day, and I was curious about how she had managed to calm Sasquatch down to a whisper.

"Can we do this outside?"

"Sure. Any reason?"

"Ain't nothing wrong with your office. But Bear and me, we likes it better outside."

I couldn't disagree. It was one of those bright, sunny days, where the sun was low in the sky and made you squint because you didn't bring sunglasses. I slipped on my jacket, and we went outside and sat on the bench in the gazebo. All the while, Bear balanced effortlessly on Traveler Jacki's shoulders.

According to Traveler Jacki, her appearance at the chapel was totally by chance. She was following up with me about bringing Bear onto the unit as a therapy animal, and when she saw people going into the Chapel, she was curious and joined the crowd.

"Can we just talk about that patient with the knife? Weren't you afraid of him?"

"Nah, not really. 'Sides, he didn't mean to kill his sister or hurt his brother. The angry spirits got to him. Like in the Chapel today. He didn't want to hurt that lady, either."

"What? How did you know about his sister and brother?"

"Well, uhm... wasn't that in the news?"

"Yeah, but, that happened years ago!"

"Bear and me, we kinda know when bad things are gonna happen," she said, nudging me in the side as Bear turned at me and showed his teeth, growling as if to depict anger. Then he yipped once and wagged his tail.

"Well then, what about the drum and the singing? Were you distracting him or what? It really quieted him down, but... I don't understand."

She answered, but the whole time she was rummaging in her backpack. "Oh. That's an ancient lullaby. A Traveler's song to the Spirits. Strong medicine puts even angry spirits to sleep."

"Angry spirits? What do you mean?"

"Spirits are just energy, Traveler Ben," she paused and looked at me. "Do you mind if I call you that? 'Sides, he looks like a Traveler, don't he, Bear?" Bear's ears perked up and he looked at me, his head tilted sideways.

"Sure, go ahead. I've been called worse."

"Like I was sayin', your patients, they ain't really sick. You just gotta remove the bad spirits, the bad energy that's got hold of 'em."

"I just... that doesn't make any sense."

"It's kinda like a fish swimming in a dirty fishbowl. A fish don't know what's makin' it sick. You gotta clean the water, Traveler Ben."

It may sound crazy, but what she said made me pause for a moment. I had often wondered if "fitting in" or being "healthy" in our culture simply meant being well-adjusted to what was at its core an unhealthy and disturbed world. Before I could respond, Traveler Jacki took a flute and hand drum out of her backpack and handed me the drum.

"Excuse me. What is this?"

"It's a drum, you silly Traveler. Let's play together. You'll learn the medicine yourself."

"Look, Traveler Jacki. This is all very nice, but it isn't really appropriate. Besides, I have work to do." Anxiously I glanced around, worried someone might see me, a psychiatric professional, engaged in some kind of spirit-chasing ritual.

"Bear, look at him. He's trying to live two breaths at a time! You can only live one breath at a time, Traveler Ben." Bear appeared to shake his head disapprovingly at me. Undaunted, Traveler Jacki started playing her flute, all the time motioning for me to join in.

The tune was mildly reminiscent of a Jethro Tull song, which brought me back to my college days when I played a Gibson six string acoustic and jammed to classic blues and rock with friends. I'd forgotten how much I had loved music, and before I knew it, I was doing my best to maintain the beat. Traveler Jacki stomped her feet as she raised the flute high in the air. As we played, I was surprised by how energized it made me feel. When my final emphatic beats brought the song to a close, Traveler Jacki sat on the ground and motioned for me to join her, which I did.

"Now. Listen. Listen," she whispered.

"Huh?" I was confused by her instruction.

"Shhhh, empty, empty." She shushed me and raised her finger to my lips. I'll admit that normally I'd have been annoyed at being shushed like a kindergartner. But Traveler Jacki's supremely kind and innocent way of acting didn't raise my defenses.

"But what am I..."

"Shhhh," she murmured again. Then, barely speaking above a whisper she said, "A full cup ain't got no space. Empty your cup, Traveler Ben. Make space to listen."

I fidgeted, trying to find a comfortable position until Traveler Jacki placed her hand on my arm. Her touch was strangely soothing, and I settled down. I listened as best I could, but the only things I heard were car tires humming on the street, a faraway siren and the muffled conversation of two passersby on the sidewalk. Impatient, I bit my lip and looked at her. Whatever was supposed to happen wasn't.

Traveler Jacki looked at me, her green eyes twinkling in the sunlight. "Breathe out the noise in your head, Traveler Ben. Breathe in the space. Let yourself grow big, bigger than the sky. Let the little body go. Let it fill with love and light."

I imagined my breath carrying my thoughts out of myself. Then I pictured breathing in space and growing myself, whatever that meant. Now it may sound strange, but I noticed a perceptible shift in awareness. Colors seemed a little more vivid; ordinary sounds faded into the background. I heard what sounded like singing, but was more like the murmur of a multi-layered chant or vibration. Suddenly, I snapped out of it, certain that what I had experienced was probably nothing more than the breeze rustling through the trees and the grass.

"He's a real fast learner, huh Bear?" Traveler Jacki grinned and Bear yelped in agreement, leaping up and licking my face.

Just then I saw Mason in the distance, walking to the front

gate with his mother and sister Dilly for his weekend visit. If I didn't know any better, I'd have thought they were a happy, contented family out for a walk. Mason saw me and waved, and I quickly stood and waved back. I wondered if he had seen me playing the drum. Slightly embarrassed, I handed the drum back to Traveler Jacki.

"Have a good weekend," I chirped, feeling somehow lighter on my feet. "See you Monday at 10:00 am for your first visit with the patients."

"Will the two-headed dragon boy be there? That was him you waved to, huh?" she asked casually.

I stopped in my tracks. "The two-headed... What on earth do you mean?"

"That boy. He's got a two-headed dragon."

It took me a moment to make the connection to Mason's dragon sketch, which David the art therapist had shown me. "That's impossible. I never told you about that..."

"See ya' right and bright at ten, Traveler Ben!" She scooted off toward the street with Bear riding shotgun on her shoulder.

All I could do was shake my head in stunned disbelief as I watched this spirited enigma leave the grounds. At least, I thought, I'd soon have my investigatory report completed. Even better, I hoped that Mason's return home would portend his release in the coming days. I'd already considered a discharge plan should that happen.

Feeling emboldened about my future prospects at the hospital, I looked forward to a stress-free weekend. Now seemed like the right time to let go of all the recent uncertainty and bizarre occurrences surrounding my work and life.

Did you ever have the sense of a new, rosier life waiting for you just around the corner? That's exactly what I felt as I drove home that night. It was literally the first time in months that a tingling of hope, excitement and anticipation accompanied me as I stepped inside my house.

Chapter 14

After settling in, I washed my face and changed into a fresh shirt before joining Beth and Judge Judy in the living room. In one hand I cradled two long-stemmed wine glasses between my fingers; in the other I held up a glistening bottle of dark red Cab. It had been a long time since I'd asked Beth to join me in what used to be a Friday evening ritual. We'd unwind and share interesting and funny stories from our respective "war zones," as we referred to our workplaces. It seemed a fitting way to end the workweek. Besides, hadn't she held my hand the other week when I sat beside her? With that in mind, I spoke with as much lyrical enticement in my voice as I could muster.

"Care to join me? We had quite the day at the clinic, with a knife-wielding psychotic and a spirit healer in the Chapel during a memorial. And, there was even talk of my getting a promotion."

Beth paused, and sat up, a little surprised. The corners of her mouth tightened for a brief moment as she thought.

"You had me at knife-wielding psychotic. It's a little chilly, but we can go outside if you're up for it."

"Sure, I'll rustle up some cheese and crackers," I said happily.

We sat in the last rays of sunshine, sipping wine and munching on Pecorino Romano, a hard cheese with sweet undertones. I can hardly describe the immense amount of pleasure—no, joy is the better word—that I felt just by sitting there and shooting the breeze with Beth. Was it mundane? Yes. Was it sublime? Yes, definitely yes.

I noticed the little things, like how she swirled the wine in her glass, how her eyes narrowed and nose crinkled to express skepticism, and how she giggled with abandon when I talked about the antics of Traveler Jacki and her shoulder-hugging dog, Bear.

I asked Beth about her week, but she didn't have much to

share, or perhaps didn't want to. Finally, I floated the idea that I might become Executive Director at the hospital, which would mean a major increase in pay.

"You could quit working. Maybe we could start doing some of the travel we talked about. We haven't traveled since, when?" I paused, remembering how our last trip had been the year before Mel's passing. The three of us went to see the Grand Canyon, which was on Mel's bucket list. I wished I hadn't mentioned it, but it was too late. Beth stiffened, set down her wine glass, and cleared her throat in a way that heralded an unwelcome announcement. She gave the wine glass a slight shove, as if to distance herself from its receptive and relaxing effects.

"I think... maybe it's time we think about separating."

To say I was stunned was putting it mildly. I set my wine glass down hard, causing it to clank loudly on the white painted metal table.

"What? I can't believe you're saying this. Why?"

"Why? I think you've made it very clear the past year."

"Oh, come on, Beth. We've both been grieving. You can't blame this on me."

"This isn't working, Benjamin. You wouldn't even go to therapy."

"Yeah, well, I wasn't ready."

"You went into a shell, Ben."

"Okay, you're right. You're right. I give you that. I was angry, okay? Maybe now, we could try to..."

"I don't think so; I don't see how."

"And you? *You're* moving on? How come I don't get a say in this? How can anything change when Mel's room remains there like some kind of hollow and empty shrine. It won't bring her back, Beth."

"Stop it. Just stop." Beth stood up, her eyes filling with tears.

I regretted my words. Worse, I hated myself for having hurt Beth. I stood and went over to her. "Beth, Beth, please. I'm sorry.

110

I never meant to shut you out."

"I know, me too." She buried her head in my chest. We stood there like that for some time, sharing a place that words were incapable of expressing. Finally, she raised her head and placed her palm gently on the side of my head.

"But please, will you think about it? I think it might be for the best."

The corners of my mouth drew downward, and I was unable to speak. With a short nod, I let go of her, and perhaps, even those dreams we had shared together over the years. After she went in the house, I stayed outside until the day-blind stars slowly shimmered to life. Sitting in darkness, I lost myself for a period of time. There was just my breath, the stars, the trees in the yard, and a tender breeze that had grown to a gust.

At some point, I became aware of a soft murmuring. I heard the sounds of voices, yet not voices, similar to my experience when I was with Traveler Jacki earlier that day. Only this time the voices didn't disappear, but increased until I sensed them more clearly now as a vibration or a hum. At the same time, I became acutely aware of multiple sensations throughout my body—the tingling of each heartbeat in my fingertips, the breath expanding and infusing my lungs, the prickliness of the chill air on every inch of my skin.

What happened next was out of the realm of my normal experience, but I'll do my best to describe it. It was as if I were experiencing my body without being *of the body*. Somehow, the ego, the person called "Ben" had vacated, leaving in its stead just spaciousness and emptiness. A paradox, to be sure, but whatever remained seemed to be a nonspecific awareness. Imagine that your awareness was expanded, like some kind of infinite balloon that extended outward to the stars, the trees, the grass. There's no longer a discrete, separate and individual *you* to be found. Instead, it's just all connecting space, and you can't tell the difference between yourself and the moon. Or between yourself and the breeze blowing through the backyard. I don't know how long I experienced this, probably only a few minutes, but it continued until the humming sound grew so loud that it shuddered me out this state, as if from a dream.

The first thing I noticed was that I was freezing, almost numb. As I rubbed my hands together they were stiff and painful. I gasped for air like a fish that had been caught on a hook and yanked from its watery home. Weakly, I stood up and stumbled inside, wondering if I'd had a convulsion or another episode of catalepsy.

Before going to bed, I put in another call to my former supervisor, Katerina, but again got her voicemail. I'm sure my voice sounded more desperate this time. The worry about my marriage and fear of losing my grip on reality kept running nonstop through my mind. I almost took an Ambien for sleep, but decided I was already far too messed up to start taking sedative hypnotic meds.

Chapter 15

I barely slept after my row with Beth. That night, the sofa bed was especially effective at twisting and digging into my ribs and lower back. I decided the best thing I could do was to get out of the house early and stay busy. Though slightly bent over with back pain, I went to the hospital to put the finishing touches on my report of Sasquatch's elopement. That meant finding out how hard it would be to get a knife from the kitchen. I conducted two experiments. Donning a bright red sweatshirt I found in my garage, I walked through the kitchen at precisely 7:00 am and noon.

These were the most hectic periods in terms of mealtime preparation. Each time, I easily found a stray carving knife and took it with me. No one greeted me or said anything. When I went back later to check in with kitchen crew, not one person remembered seeing anyone in a red sweatshirt. I concluded that Sasquatch had gone in and grabbed that carving knife without being noticed. From there, it was a short walk to the side door into the Chapel. In fact, that was the only door that had open access from that hallway.

My report, which I finished writing that afternoon in

my office, concluded that Sasquatch simply left the unit by following a food cart, going into the kitchen to get a knife, and then entering the Chapel via an unlocked side door. Traveler Jacki was there to speak with me about her pet therapy job and totally by chance followed other mourners into the Chapel. Jacki and her dog distracted and confused Sasquatch, thus allowing the orderlies to get close enough to administer an IM and get him under control.

Further, I recommended that all orderlies and staff should be trained to make sure no patients were close by when leaving the unit. Nurses would tighten their handoff process to minimize miscommunication, and a lock would need to be installed on the side Chapel door. Lastly, all chef's knives were to be relocated to a locked case where they were to be checked out whenever in use by the cooks. All in all, I was rather proud of the report, hoping it reflected the kind of leadership qualities expected of an Executive Director. I put the report in a manila envelope and hand-delivered it to Dr. Howell's mail slot.

By the end of the day, still not ready to return home, my mind was besieged by distressing thoughts that chipped away at my sense of security. If Beth and I split up, where would I go? What would happen to the house? What would be the financial consequences? Who would get which friends? I didn't mean to get cynical, but I'd seen this happen before. It felt like a train wreck about to happen, and I couldn't prevent it. Or, maybe the wreck had already happened?

With these thoughts endlessly jabbing at me, I seriously considered using the white board in my own office to complete a cognitive behavioral worksheet. Certainly, there must be a balanced view that I could find here? Or, at least some evidence that refuted my unfounded beliefs? I guess I could have done that, but it seemed better, maybe easier, to go outside and distract myself by thinking about where the hospital's new expansion would take place. Don't underrate distraction as a therapy tool.

Walking the grounds, I suddenly realized the expansion would destroy much of the lush greenery that warmed the otherwise sterile building. Several mature maple, aspen and oak trees would need to be removed, as would the topiary shrubbery, gazebo and garden. Slowly, I meandered over to the stone cottage where Reggie had lived. A light green moss had taken up residence on the stone pathway leading to the front door. That's when I noticed that the front door was slightly ajar. I walked up and gingerly pushed on it. Instantly, I noticed a burning smell as a wisp of smoke escaped. Fearing fire, I quickly kicked at the door, swinging it wide open.

"Eiiyee!!" I shouted involuntarily. In the dim light, someone was huddled in the center of the room, starting a fire. Hijacked by fear, I backed out, ready to make a run for it. "I'm going to call security, so you better get out of here. This is private property!"

I ran toward the hospital to get hold of a security officer. But I'd hardly gone a few steps when something grabbed my pants. I looked down and saw Bear tugging at my cuff. When I stopped, he let go and ran back toward the stone cottage. Like a herding dog, he barked and looked back at me, as if waiting for me to follow him. After following Bear inside the cottage, it took a few moments before my eyes adjusted to the darkness. All I could detect was the sound of a guttural voice singing something unintelligible.

What I'd mistaken for a fire, I now realized, were actually burning embers contained in a small bowl. Traveler Jacki moved about the room while repeating some words over and over, a mantra perhaps? She held above her head what looked like a small stalk of burning embers. The end of the stalk was glowing red as she waved it in a circular fashion, spreading smoke all around. She continued like this until the whole cottage smelled of burnt sage and cedar. When finished, she set down the bundle and extinguished it in the bowl. She intoned a few final words while turning in each of four directions, which seemed to coordinate with east, south, west and north. Only after placing her hands over her heart center did she greet me.

"Thank you for joining in our space clearing, Traveler Ben."

"Well, I didn't so much join you as stumble on you. Which, by the way, scared the daylights out of me. And what's a space clearing?"

"Negative energy. With Reggie dying here, it needed to be cleansed. Can you feel the difference?"

"Yeah, it's smoky, if that's what you mean."

"It's called smudging. Gets the energy movin'."

"Jacki, even if that's a good thing, you broke in here, and that's a bad thing."

"No, Bear found a key." She proudly held the key between her fingertips. "It was under the mat."

"Okay, well I suppose if you just clean up and take all your smoke accoutrements with you, no one will be the wiser."

"Traveler Ben, can I ask a big favor? Could me and Bear stay here for a bit?"

"Where? Here, in the cottage?"

"Just for a bit. I can do the landscaping. Look outside." She pointed in the direction of the flower beds.

What I was seeing took a while to sink in. The flowers, which were ready to expire just a couple of days earlier, were now blooming. In fact, I it looked like there were many more flowers along the fence than I'd ever seen. Even Reggie would have been impressed.

"When... when did you find the time to plant all this?"

"Please, let us stay?"

"I'll look into it. I'm not promising anything. And I'm sure it will only be temporary. At best."

Instead of having Traveler Jacki go through Human Resources, which I was pretty certain wouldn't go over very well, I decided to handle matters directly. I went to see Beverly, who was working late. I'd barely taken a step inside when she held up a familiar looking manila envelope.

"Just finished reading it, Ben. Your report." Beverly's eyes narrowed.

I stopped in my tracks, holding my breath for the verdict.

"It's excellent and very thorough. Absolutely perfect for what I need," she said, smiling broadly.

I grinned, relieved. "I didn't think you'd get to it so fast. I'm really glad you liked it." Given Beverly's upbeat demeanor, I figured now was as good a time as any to ask about Traveler Jacki staying in the cottage. Beverly readily agreed, but only on the stipulation that Jacki provide references for working as a gardener.

As soon as I left Beverly's office, I began to question my judgment. This itinerant woman and her pet were just too unpredictable, especially with my opportunity to become Executive Director hanging in the balance. By the time I returned, Jacki was making the cottage her home, busily arranging the contents of her backpack on a small table. I was all set to explain why her staying wasn't a good idea when she ran over and gave me a big hug.

"Bless you, Traveler Ben! Me and Bear, we ain't had a home in so long."

"Not so fast, that's not exactly what I was going to say."

"What do you mean?"

When I saw Bear yawn, stretch his legs and curl up on the blanket, I felt my stance softening. "Well, the thing is... you need gardening references. And it's only temporary."

"Pretty sure I got a reference in here somewhere." She fumbled inside her backpack.

"Really? Tell me something. How come everything you need seems to magically appear out of there? That's kind of outlandish, right?"

"Yeah, give me a sec."

"Oh, what the hell. Just don't kill any plants out there, okay? The tool shed is around the side of the building. I'll tell security to give you access."

Leaving the cottage, I wondered how I had gotten entangled with this seemingly psychic, ritual loving woman and her highly sentient dog. While I liked helping people from a therapy perspective, I'd grown aloof in my personal life—especially after Mel's death.

My friends had gone on living, engaged in their children's lives. It's not that I didn't care, but I found it difficult to hear about their children, who were graduating, getting jobs, getting married, starting families. And so, gatherings became more and more awkward, filled with a stifling vacancy. After a while they stopped asking how I was doing with the loss, and I never shared. Now, a year later, all communication had downsized to the dribble of a rare email.

Or, had I simply hidden behind my therapeutic embrace of objectivity and non-disclosure for so long, that it finally crept into all areas of my life? Maybe that's why Mason had upset me—he had pierced my personal veil and peered into my private life and loss.

I had often reflected on the origins of psychotherapy and Freud. The practice of sitting behind patients was meant to facilitate free association. But being invisible as someone spilled out their inner fears, dreams and desires, somehow felt haughty, detached and voyeuristic. I have always tried to listen, to be empathic, to be authentic. And yet, wasn't even prescribing medication a form of stepping up on a pedestal? Maybe it was time to step down from my own high horse. After all, was it really so bad to get involved and get your hands dirty with life's grittiness?

Whenever I thought of grit, I was reminded of Herman, a patient of mine years ago, whose acute depression and lack of self-esteem seemed entwined. He thought lowly of himself for working in the trades, as if his status as a human being was measured by his education and job. And yet, this man made some fifty sandwiches each Saturday morning and drove them down to a destitute neighborhood in Portland. From the trunk of his car, he handed out sandwiches and bottled water to the less fortunate.

Herman's selfless behavior, his grit in spite of his own struggles, left me in awe and earned him my deep admiration. While I thought I'd never do anything like that, my actions on behalf of Traveler Jacki had taken me out of my comfort zone and far beyond my psychiatrist's role—not to mention breaking all kinds of hospital and hiring protocols. But seeing how happy it made Traveler Jacki and Bear, it was well worth the effort.

I walked over to a local grocery mart and picked up some staples—milk, eggs and bread, and oh yes, dog food—and set two brown bags down by the cottage door. Sometimes, as I had often advised patients, helping others is the best way of helping yourself. Maybe that's why I left the hospital that day feeling better than I had in a while.

Chapter 16

On Sunday, Beth and I tiptoed around each other at home. I'd make breakfast, then she'd make breakfast. She'd bring wood in for the fire, then I'd bring wood in for the fire. We were like two people invisibly inhabiting the same space. It was like that movie *Interstellar*, where the main character could clearly see into another dimension, but was unable to touch or communicate with it. It was damn frustrating, and I was about to go out of my mind until I got a phone call from Katerina. She had returned from giving a workshop in Budapest and could see me that afternoon.

Driving to Portland's Pearl District, or "the Pearl," reminded me of other big cities I'd visited. Unlike the sedate surroundings of my suburban home, the Pearl was the hub of all things artsy and trendy. It was literally teeming with the city's best eateries, boutiques, coffee houses and art galleries. The Pearl was within walking distance of the Portland Art Museum and the Oregon Historical Society. And if you liked jazz and were lucky, there was always a chance you could find a club featuring Mel Brown, a legendary figure in the Rose City jazz scene. But good luck finding a parking spot.

I had visited Katerina's condo more than once. Soon after my supervision with her ended, our working relationship transitioned into a friendship. I'd always counted on Katerina's no-nonsense ability to zero in on any issue. I still consulted with her on some befuddling cases, but also whenever I faced a roadblock in my own life. Katerina was never phony. She always said that being inauthentic was not just a waste of time, but a waste of life. Whatever wisdom she had gained in her life must have been hard earned, though she rarely spoke of it.

Katerina always sidestepped any talk about her time in New York as a dancer, when she had performed with Baryshnikov and had a promising career that was cut short due to injury. She only obliquely referred to her time as a seeker in India, where she lived for a period of time in an ashram as a disciple of a well-known Indian Hindu sage. Which one, however, she would not reveal.

Whenever she shared these tidbits, I would be simultaneously enthralled and repulsed. In comparison, my life was paint-by-numbers trajectory. I went from high school to college to medical school without stopping to take a breath or consider other alternatives. Even in my marriage, Beth was always the one who wanted to travel and seek adventure; I resisted anything that strayed too far from the known and the ordinary. Maybe that's why I always found Katerina's bohemian style of living and therapy so intriguing.

Yes, I did visit Katerina during the time when Mel was going through chemo, but I hadn't seen her since the memorial service. Katerina had stopped working as a psychotherapist, but she continued traveling the world and teaching workshops on what she called "spiritual relationships." This was the first time I'd been to her home since her partner, Kasimir, a gentle painter and poet, had passed.

I checked in with the doorman, who dutifully reminded me of Katerina's floor number and which direction to turn off the elevator. When Katerina opened the door, she smiled broadly, arms open wide. As we hugged, I felt welcomed and accepted in a way that I very much needed in the moment.

"Hi, kiddo! Great to see you!"

"How long's it been?" I asked, even though I knew.

"Too long. You're looking good." She stepped back to absorb my essence in a head-to-toe gestalt kind of way.

"You too." I looked at her, marveling at her sense of flair. Over her willowy and lithe body she wore a flowing, floor-length black silk sari embroidered with golden lotus flowers and delicately curled shapes. Around her neck hung several long strands of round jade gemstones, punctuated with a carved jade rose dangling at the bottom.

"Don't try to fool me, kiddo. I've entered my crone years," she countered with a short cackle.

I smiled at her reference. A crone, after all, was an archetype representing the winter season of life, the rich culmination of what maidenhood and motherhood brought to bear on this last of life's cycles. Although it was evident Katerina had once been a stunningly beautiful woman, even in her 70s she still maintained that *je ne sais quoi* sparkle.

Katerina hung my jacket on the black coat stand and led the way into the living room, almost appearing to float across the glossy, dark stained hardwood floor. The living room walls were splashed with colorful, light-hearted sketches from Dalí and Chagall, who were her favorite artists. Between two upright and thickly upholstered maroon chairs, an elegant, porcelain tea service awaited us. Katerina poured my tea, then her own. She sat sipping hers and not saying a word, courteously giving me time to collect my thoughts. I could feel myself coming into the moment as I swirled the hot reddish liquid in my mouth, tasting subtle hints of licorice and rosebuds.

I wasn't sure where to begin, and the story of my personal and work life collided clumsily in the telling. I apologized more than once when I didn't feel like I was making any sense, but Katerina didn't buy my nonsense.

"Don't apologize, Ben. You know what you're feeling, what you're up against. Tell your truth."

I nodded and continued, letting the story spill out of me, at first slow and thick, but then flowing easily like warmed maple syrup. My renderings of Mason and Jacki, the twin Travelers who entered my life at almost the same time, instantly stirred Katerina's curiosity.

"Travelers," interjected Katerina, "What a marvelous name for the unknown and the mystery in all of us."

"But Mason doing the out-of-body thing? And Jacki intuiting the dragon painting?"

"Ben," she smiled, almost coquettishly, "you know there are ways of accessing information that we cannot fully understand. When I was in India, for example, my teacher knew things about me that were impossible for anyone to know."

"Like what?"

"For one, he knew the exact time that my mother died back in the States, and I didn't even know she was ill or in the hospital. It made me realize that there were other ways of seeing and knowing. Tell me, have you heard of Vivekananda?"

I paused, shaking my head. "Was that your teacher in the ashram?"

"No. Vivekananda was a great spiritual teacher, and one of the first to come to the West from India in the nineteenth century." Katerina leaned toward me, speaking barely above a whisper and forcing me to listen. Her pupils enlarged, becoming black and empty. It seemed as if she was looking through me as she said, *The infinite library of the universe is in your own mind.*

The words literally penetrated me, and I almost imagined this nineteenth-century Indian sage sitting there. My neck felt prickly and a shiver spread down my arms.

"There's a vast, untapped dimension that is available to us,

Ben. Maybe you're being asked to step into it?" Katerina stood up and went to a large wooden bookcase. She knew exactly where to reach for a small book. "Do you know of St. Thomas Aquinas?"

"I remember reading him for a college philosophy class. But that's literally all I remember."

Katerina returned to her chair, opening the book as if it were a delicate work of art. She spoke in a soft, yet sonorous, voice:

"The activity of understanding is wholly non-material. The act of understanding is not an action of the body or of any bodily energy. Hence to be joined to a body is not the essence of intellectual being. So, What do you think?"

I felt like I was back in school, when I didn't understand Aquinas the first time around. "I'm not sure. I mean, if the intellect doesn't need a body, then what does that mean?"

She glanced back at the book.

"Not all intellects are conjoined with bodies; there are some that exist separately, and these we call angels."

Katerina looked up at me, awaiting my pearls of wisdom. Unfortunately, I could find none. "Uhm, you mean like the chubby cherubs in those pictures?"

Katerina stifled a smile. "Not quite. Maybe angels are really a powerful energy source we communicate with using intuition and inspiration. They act as catalysts, and may even be guides who take us beyond our six senses."

"You mean like a guardian angel who comes to your aid, like a personal servant? Kind of narcissistic, isn't it?"

"That's perfect for our selfie-obsessed culture!" After a short cackle, she continued. "But I'm thinking broader context. The mystical or magical, in whatever form it takes, guides us to a more inventive and fertile understanding of things, don't you think? Didn't you say Mason's experience gave him a sense of relief by knowing there was something beyond the mundane world in which he was stuck?"

"It certainly seemed that way."

"Visions are not always delusions and hallucinations generated by the brain. For example, Aquinas says that the energy of angels is penetrating. It flows into everything, even the smallest blade of grass."

"That's just... Sorry, but this is a little too New Age for me, Katerina."

"Let me ask you. Would you say it's *possible* Mason is being guided by an intelligent energy? And is it harming him or hurting him?"

"You have a point there. Whatever it is, it's not hurting him. Or harming others."

"I know documented cases of schizophrenia that have been recognized as enlightenment experiences."

"Tell me. Can this energy come in human form?"

"Sure. I don't see why not."

"But didn't Aquinas say that angels don't exist in material form?"

"Yes, but they can *appear* to be physical, in the same way that a hologram appears to be."

"Oh God, I can't believe we're talking about angels!" I shifted uncomfortably in my chair, as if mirroring the discomfort in my mind.

"Ben, this conversation wouldn't have been unusual in Aquinas' time."

"True, but we're not in the Middle Ages." Though I refrained from rolling my eyes, I'm afraid that I bit my lip. It all seemed so incredulous.

"Divine silence. That might be why we don't hear or see them anymore."

"Huh?"

"Our world. It's buzzing. Electronic waves feed us a constant stream of static. Every time you're distracted and hijacked from the present moment, you lose a part of your soul and divine self. Without silence there's no way to tap into awe, magic and wonder. Divine silence, Ben."

As Katerina spoke, I thought back on how Traveler Jacki had tried to teach me about being silent. Truth was, I had no clue how to connect with my own wife, let alone a dimension of the divine. But Katerina had struck a nerve because I realized then how much I feared silence. I had kept silence at bay by endlessly reading and answering work emails, keeping up with scads of journal articles, and staying forever distracted. This helped me avoid the puzzle of my own grief over the loss of my daughter that I couldn't solve.

"Ben?" said Katerina, with a concerned expression on her face.

"Sorry, I drifted off."

"Where did you go?"

"I was thinking about how I use distraction to avoid silence, and to keep me from facing difficult issues in my life." That's when I finally told Katerina that Beth wanted to separate. I felt tears in the corners of my eyes, and I wiped them away.

"Oh, Ben, I'm so sorry." Katerina placed a hand over her heart. She leaned forward and asked, friend to friend, "How are you doing?"

"Not too good, I'm afraid." As I shared the story, I wondered if even a wise crone could make sense of it all.

"You know what this is all about, don't you, Ben?" I sat there without moving a muscle as Katerina paused for a long beat. Then, in a most gentle voice she continued, "This is about faith, kiddo. Your faith, or rather, lack of it."

"Faith? I'm not sure I understand." I shifted nervously as Katerina's brown eyes burrowed into me like lasers.

"You might think of it as a willingness to open up to the mystery... to the unknown. The impossible. To whatever it is that you can't grasp or know." Her dark eyebrows raised up as she said, "You're holding on too tightly, Ben. That's the controlling mind, the controlling ego."

I sighed deeply, letting go my tension. "Yeah, yeah, yeah. You're right. I'm holding on. But who wants to live in a world where anything goes?" I paused, reflecting on what I'd just said. Damn, what *part of me*, to use Internal Family Systems lingo, sounded like a mash-up of pop lyrics? I was about to continue, when I noticed that Katerina was gazing at me with a soft, tender and bemused expression. Unexpectedly, I flashed back to when Mel was only seven and asked me about the birds and the bees. How could I explain it to her at that age? That's when I had looked at her with that same soft gaze of love, knowing that one day she'd get the answers that were now beyond her grasp. Is that what Katerina thought of me—that I was a little puppy dog and this was beyond my grasp? What if she was right?

I leaned toward Katerina, ready to listen, *really* listen. "Okay, I can see that, Katerina... my mind wanting to be in control. But people don't appear on a rooftop while they're in bed sleeping. Do they? That's just wrong."

"Ben, it's okay to doubt. But use your doubt to look further, to question. Did you know that bi-location was common at the time of the Buddha? Monks were taught how to do this. Saint Francis, St. Thomas Aquinas and others were seen levitating." When I didn't say anything for a few seconds, her expression turned into what looked like a frown.

"Let me get this straight. Are you saying... that my patient is seeing an angel? Or that this homeless lady and her dog are a manifestation of God knows what?"

"No, Ben, that's not what I'm saying at all. I'm just saying there's the *possibility* that the improbable... or what we call miracles... can happen."

"All right. Supposing that were true, how would that change anything?"

"Ben, are you willing to try an experiment?"

"Sure." I adjusted my posture, sitting upright. I wondered if she was going to use any number of techniques for patients who were stuck in rigid thinking styles. But her instructions took me by surprise.

"For the next few minutes, Ben, I want you to revisit Traveler Jacki telling you about contacting spirits, and Mason telling you about traveling out of his body. Only this time, I want you to sense and experience these stories with your body, not your mind or head. Sit with the experience until it's as real as the feeling of rubbing your palms together or knowing that the sky is blue. In fact, let's begin by rubbing your palms together for a few seconds."

For a moment I was confused. How was that even possible? I'd attended some body-related workshops, but they were focused on trauma.

After rubbing my palms together, Katerina continued, "Yes, Ben, there is a way to understand any event by tapping how your *body* interprets it. You'll be opening to a new understanding that is beyond mental concepts or words. If you notice any words or thoughts trying to shape the story, just let these go. Now, give yourself time to sit with these happenings. You might even picture breathing the events into your body, letting them enter you through the breath."

I followed her instructions and sat with the conundrum of absorbing into my body things that my mind had already decided were "impossible." Was this easy for me to do? No, definitely not. But something happened that I'd never experienced before. After several minutes, a deep sentience poured over me, or should I say "into me." It was a kind of knowing which cannot be described with words. But it was deeply liberating, because it subverted any interference from my personal history that colored my beliefs, stories and narratives. All I knew, deep down, was that, yes, the things that Traveler Jacki and Mason described *could* be true. There was that strong possibility. *Damn.* At that moment, I looked up at Katerina, flabbergasted.

"Did you hypnotize me?" I asked, only half facetiously.

"Good, something happened. Now tell me. What changed?"

"It feels crazy but… but when I felt the truth of those kinds of things happening…"

"Yes, go on…"

"I knew there must still be miracles. Somewhere. Somehow. It made sense when viewed through the feelings of the body. It was, I don't know… somehow affirming."

"And what does that mean for you?"

"I'd like to bi-locate to Hawaii for the winter?" I deadpanned, raising my eyebrows.

"Always the kidder," Katerina said with a wink. "You sit with that knowing. I'll be right back."

She left the room while I considered the deeper implications of allowing for what seemed to be impossible. In a comforting way, I felt like Katerina had reawakened my interest and curiosity in the mystical side of things. I sat there with a sense of anticipation for what it would be like to open the "doors of perception," as Aldous Huxley referred to it. What concerned me, however, was that I'd already begun to open that door. And it frightened me.

When Katerina returned, she held a small blue tin on which was painted a picture of the world.

"Here," she whispered, pressing the metal tin into my palm as if it held something very precious.

"What is it?" I started to pry open the tin.

"Not yet, Ben."

"Huh?"

"Only open it when you're ready to face your deepest fear. But only when you're a hundred percent ready. Promise me."

"Promise." I closed my fingers around the little box. "But how will I know when…"

"Trust me, you'll know. In the meantime, kiddo, start by finding more silence."

Driving home, I kept wondering if what Katerina had said was right. Were my own fear and need for control blocking me from a deeper truth? One thing was for certain. What I was doing wasn't working.

Or, as some therapists liked to ask their patients: "How's that working for you?" I've never been so crass as to ask anyone that because it stinks of superiority. But it seemed that Katerina just did ask me that, in her own way, and judging by how I felt, it was effective at getting me to reconsider things.

I remembered reading how even Einstein couldn't understand how particles could be entangled at a distance, and so he had mocked it as "spooky action at a distance." Maybe I just needed to admit that the Universe was large enough to keep a spooky mystery or two from us humans. Rationality and logic expressed only one part of the story.

In my newfound effort to see things differently, I took a detour home, which took me past the hospital. It was Sunday evening, and the streets were empty, so I sat in my car, just reflecting on the past events. Finally, I smiled thinking of the time Mason told me in session to "go home and chill." That was exactly what I'd try to do.

Only, I never did make it home.

Chapter 17

I kept staring up at the roof where I'd seen Mason sitting. Despite my best attempts to remain open to *possibility*, my rational mind kept hunting for a more suitable answer. At one point, I almost concluded that it must have been *my* hallucination—except that Mason said he heard me calling him. In that case, I wondered if it was a shared delusional disorder, or *folie à deux*, which roughly translates as "madness for two." Such were my mental ramblings when I noticed a shadowy figure moving haltingly around the hospital grounds. Whoever it was appeared to be swinging something back and forth in the air.

As quietly as possible, I climbed out of my car and squatted down to stay out of sight. When I reached the gated entrance, I took out my phone in case I needed to call for help. The figure came in and out of view as I followed it, using trees as cover. At some point, however, it disappeared altogether. After I looked around quietly for a couple of minutes, I decided to continue this surveillance from the safety of my car. But when I turned around, a distorted face, like something out of a zombie or slasher movie (take your pick) appeared just a foot away, illuminated in light.

With a gasp I jolted backwards, unceremoniously slipping and falling on my backside. "What the...?" I said, looking up at Traveler Jacki, who was holding a flashlight under her chin for a horror-inducing effect. She was chuckling, which made me angrier. I stood up, rubbing the wet mud off my pants and jacket, which only spread the muck. "Traveler Jacki? Geez, you scared the hell out of me!"

"I'm sorry. But you scared me first. I saw you following me."

"What are you doing out here in the dark?" I noticed that she was holding a long branch in one hand. It had something long and shiny secured to one end with rubber bands.

"Oh nothing. Me and Bear, we likes our evening walks." She tried to hide the contraption behind her back.

"Come on, what are you not telling me? What is that thing?" Traveler Jacki held my gaze for a long time, as if she were pondering whether to share something with me.

"Like I said, it ain't nothin'."

"I need you to be honest with me, okay? I put myself on the line by having you work here and stay in the cottage."

"You ain't gonna believe it no how."

"Try me. I'm actually a lot more open to things than you might think. Very open. Very, very, uhm, open."

"It's a crystal. I tied it to this twig so I can listen better." Traveler Jacki held it in front of me so I could take a better look.

"Okay. Tell me more."

"Crystals, you see, they're like the Earth's antennas. They pick up the smallest signals." She raised the slender green-gold quartz higher. "It will move in a direction when it picks up a signal."

"Still, I feel like you're not really telling me what's going on here."

"Okay, Traveler Ben," she said, pausing for a long time. "The real reason we came here is because of the spirits."

"Okay, I'm listening. What about the spirits?"

134

"Me and Bear, we heard 'em calling for help."

"Who? The patients in the hospital?"

"No, no, no. The Old Ones. The ancient Travelers. They say there's a treasure buried here. Me and Bear gotta find it before it's too late."

"A treasure. You're absolutely sure?" Despite my wanting to forego doubt, the psychiatrist in me, a well-entrenched part of my identity, took over.

"Yeah, it's near here. That's what they told us, right, Bear?"

I shuffled my feet uncomfortably. "Look, Traveler Jacki, I want to believe you, really… I do. But there's no treasure here, okay? Whatever it is you think you're hearing, you can't make things reality just because…"

"But the spirits, they need our help," she urgently interrupted.

"I don't care if you're getting messages from the tooth fairy or that feather in your hair, but let's stop pretending there's a treasure, okay?" Traveler Jacki's expression wilted, and her posture slumped.

"See, I knew it," she said, lowering her crystal antenna, looking hurt. "Me and Bear, I guess we was wrong about you. I think it best we be going." Jacki trudged toward the cottage, with Bear blithely prancing alongside.

Immediately, I regretted my words and wished I could take them back. This kindly woman, who I knew would never hurt anyone, didn't deserve my rebuke. Worse, I felt like I had just stuck a pin in the balloon of my desire to explore the mystical side of being. "Oh, shit," I thought to myself, "maybe you just can't teach an old dog new tricks." I let go a long breath of resignation and shook my head to no one in particular.

Standing alone in the darkness, I felt myself slipping into the abyss of despair that I'd known during Mel's last days. If only Mel was here now, I wished. That's when the most improbable thing occurred. Mel's bird, that elusive American Goldfinch, flapped down from above, circled around me three or four times, and then alighted on my shoulder. It chirped excitedly, tilting its black and golden head toward me. I watched in astonishment as it inched up my shoulder to get closer to my face. As I swiveled my head to face it, its tiny black eyes glowed in the moonlight. I raised my hand slowly, and the little creature allowed me to stroke its head and back.

That's when I felt a barely discernible sensation in my heart. It was like an ache, but also a feeling of warmth. It took me a while to grasp what was happening until an image appeared in my mind's eye. I pictured my heart surrounded by armor, and the armor had started to soften. It was just melting away, and I could feel this incredible warmth spreading through my chest.

The finch and I communed like this until, trembling, I felt tears running down my cheeks. Then, the bird's black wings ever-so-gently fluttered and brushed against my face, wiping away the tears. It looked up and gave my finger a playful nip with its beak, holding onto me for a moment. Finally, with what sounded like a chirp of joy, it leapt into the moonlit sky. I followed it for as long as I could, until its diminutive shape melted into black.

I caught my breath and placed a hand over my heart. There was still a deep sadness, but the blockage of anger and torment that I'd lived with began to ebb. Though I couldn't fathom how, I knew I had been contacted by Melissa.

The event had completely circumvented my logical mindset and my years of therapeutic training. "This is exactly what Katerina was talking about," I pondered excitedly, still peering up into the sky, which seemed to open up wide. Suddenly, the mundane world appeared gilded and ablaze. It was in that moment I thought, "Why not a treasure, here on the hospital's own grounds?"

Moments later, defying my years of training, I rushed over to the cottage and knocked on the half-opened door. Traveler Jacki was almost done packing up her meager belongings.

"Traveler Jacki, wait."

"For what?"

"I'm really sorry." I tried to make eye contact, but she kept packing.

"Don't matter none."

"No, really," I pleaded, "Please... hear me out."

"Some things, they just ain't meant to be." She zipped up her backpack, then picked up something from the table. "Here. I made this for you, Traveler Ben. I was gonna give it to you tomorrow."

In my palm she placed a wire-wrapped necklace. At the bottom hung an oval-shaped pendant that held a dazzling pink stone. Normally, I'd have refused the gift, which is what we're trained to do as therapists. However, I felt it that in this case, it would be unkind not to accept it.

"It's gorgeous! Thank you. You didn't need to do this."

"It's rose quartz. Give it to someone you love. Like maybe... aww, you know who." Traveler Jacki lifted Bear onto her shoulder and stepped out the door. I scuttled along behind.

"Traveler Jacki, wait. You can't go. I want you to teach me."

"Huh? Teach you what?"

"About the, uhm... the spirits. How to hear them. I just want to learn. Will you help me? Please."

Traveler Jacki finally stopped and turned to me with a serious expression. She looked at me in silence for a few moments. "You sure? You really wanna learn the way of the Traveler? It ain't so easy."

"Yeah, I'm sure."

"I thought you would!" She wore the biggest grin I'd seen in a long time. We both started laughing, although I had no idea what kind of mess I'd gotten myself into.

Traveler Jacki decided we shouldn't waste any time. We'd begin my training immediately. Besides, I had no other obligations on Sunday evening. When I asked how long it would take for me to hear the spirits, she only smiled and said, "Takes a whiles." Then she told me about a way of seeing that most people never knew about.

This *Traveler's eye*, or *second seeing*, as she also called it, was not the same as ordinary awareness. Traveler Jacki explained how *Traveler's eye* allowed her to see the illness in Sasquatch. Likewise, she told me how she literally *saw* the double-headed dragon in Mason when he was walking with his family.

"So, you weren't talking about his painting?"

"Nah, the dragon is a spirit attached to him, hurting him." When I told Traveler Jacki that Mason had drawn a picture of his own dragons, her response was that, "He got the gift of seeing." A few, she said, were born with the gift and were destined to become healers. She was very interested in meeting with Mason at our pet therapy group the next morning.

I expected Jacki to lead me through a breathing meditation, but she said that I needed to take a real journey first, in order to learn to *see*.

"Where? Around the neighborhood? I'm ready."

"Truth is, Traveler Ben, I'm kinda worried. I didn't tell you but..."

"Tell me what?"

"Once you see like a Traveler, there ain't no turning back. Your life won't ever be the same. Bear knows this, too." Bear put his head on the ground and covered his eyes with his paws.

I'd never seen Traveler Jacki this solemn. She evidently felt my misgivings, and so she was giving me the chance to back out. "I see what you mean. What do you suggest?"

"Tells you what. I can show you what it's like to really *see*, Traveler Ben. You'll see what I see, but only once. Then you decide."

My settled, predictable *way of living* was on the line. But on the other hand, I felt as if my ability to really *live* was also at stake. What if I never had this chance again?

"Okay, let's do it." I gulped, not sure what was going to happen next.

"Take a deep breath. Relax and let go." Slowly, Traveler Jacki brought her head closer to mine. Her eyes glimmered like two dark emeralds in the moonlight. Then, her forehead touched mine.

An instantaneous jolt of electricity surged through my entire body. My first instinct was to pull back, but I remained stationary as she continued touching my forehead for about a minute. When she separated from me, I had the sense of a completely different consciousness, one totally foreign from my own. It was something right out of the series *Star Trek*, where Spock used his Vulcan Mind Meld to create one mind from two. This was not my reality, but the reality of Traveler Jacki. I was, quite literally, *out of my mind*. Looking back, I know that if I had been unstable, I might have never recovered from this *mindjack*. I'd heard of Tibetan Lamas who transferred consciousness in this way, but I never really believed it until now.

Being inside another's mental awareness was simultaneously horrifying and astonishing. My body appeared to glow with spurts of energy that extended outward. I was at once struck by how expansive I felt. That's when I realized I couldn't sense my skin, which was followed by the shocking realization that there was no longer a distinct boundary separating my individual self from its surroundings.

Looking around, I witnessed an indescribably brilliant and vitally alive landscape. Every tree, leaf, flower and thing pulsated with waves of energy in different colors. Bursts of red, green, blue and yellow energy from trees spread out in spiral plumes; I felt their peacefulness infuse and mix with my own plumes of energy. It seemed as if solid matter had been unfrozen and thawed out to become living light. Whatever doubts I had held about the existence of other realities and ways of knowing dissolved then and there.

I thought I heard Traveler Jacki say, "Follow me," but I swear her mouth didn't move. I followed behind, watching in amazement as every person nearby glowed as an energy body. Some had wispy energies, like smoke, that floated above their heads. Were these the "spirits" she had talked about? I was shocked to see a turbulent red and black mass hovering beside a man who moved furtively. I avoided his dark stare and quickly veered out of his path.

We approached an aging woman in tattered clothes. She was immersed in the most sublime, almost angelic white light. I could feel the cool mist of her tenderness and love surrounding me as she passed by. This enhanced Traveler's eye soon faded, and the living light became frozen and solid again. As we walked back to the cottage, I couldn't speak. I was flummoxed and feeling like I had just been inside a surrealistic painting. Only this painting revealed the subtle energetic forces that animated our lives.

My mind whirled with ideas. I questioned whether energy could be intentionally transmitted outward in order to change how others felt, thought and behaved. To do that would be like an energetic form of cognitive behavioral therapy. Slyly, I glanced over at Traveler Jacki. Could she shift the energy patterns of others? If so, the Traveler's eye was a powerful gift. But it all seemed to come down to one thing:

Could I handle this?

"Traveler Jacki, will I see this all the time?"

"No, you silly Traveler. Some never get that far. But over time you'll see more. Traveler's eye, it ain't for everyone. It takes a strong heart, and Traveler Ben, you got that. Don't he, Bear?"

Bear leapt up into my arms, something that he had never done before. He stared into my eyes for a long time.

"Well, if Bear thinks I'm ready," I said, rubbing Bear under the chin.

Traveler Jacki explained that first I needed to find my spirit guide. The guide would protect me, as well as help me learn to use my Traveler's eye. She had me lie down on the grass near the cottage and close my eyes. I was instructed to ask the "ancient and distant Travelers" for guidance, and to pay attention to any images that came to me. In the meantime, Traveler Jacki went into the cottage to prepare a special herbal remedy she said would help me.

I was lying there for a few minutes when I heard the gentle beating of a hand drum. Then I heard Traveler Jacki's voice, speaking to me softly.

"Trust in the ancient Old Ones, the old Travelers, who have been to this world and beyond many times. Let them guide you on this spirit journey."

Slowly, Traveler Jacki started drumming faster on her hand drum. She told me to look for a tunnel or entrance to the deep "world below." I wasn't sure if it was the trance-inducing beat of the drum, but I saw something that looked like a large gaping knot in a tree. I decided to see if I could go down that hole. Surprisingly, I entered and slid down into a large tunnel. While sliding downward, I had to twist and turn to avoid outcroppings of earth, roots, and rocks. But it was pretty easy to avoid them even in what was a dim, diffused glow.

Finally, I reached the floor, or bottom. Looking around, I realized I was in a massive cavern, damp and cool. I followed a pathway at one end of the cavern, walking past gurgling pools and gargoyle-looking formations. When the passage became narrow and sinuous I started worrying if I would find the way out. Just then, I turned a corner where light streamed in from a large opening. I could feel myself sigh a deep sense of relief.

I still heard the drumming from a faraway distance. The beating drum was felt like a heartbeat safely connecting me back to my presence and my body up above. This hardly seemed like a fantasy to me anymore.

"What am I looking for?" I asked. I'm pretty sure I didn't say these words aloud.

"Ask to meet your spirit guardian. You will know it," responded a calming voice.

As I stepped through the opening, I stood on a vast and hilly landscape that was rich in shades of purple, green, red, and brown, draped over one another like fabrics of silk and satin. The sun, which resembled a spiraling galaxy, was soft and muted, and I could feel an openness, where anything seemed possible. As I continued to ask for my guardian spirit, the sky along the horizon darkened with gray rain clouds. Droplets of water touched the earth, and then these moving droplets were approaching me at a dizzying speed.

When they got close enough for me to start getting wet, I realized that this was not a rain cloud at all, but a downpour of butterflies. A lepidopterist's dream drenched me in a colorful butterfly bubble. They landed all over me, on my head, my nose, my legs, my feet, my arms. I held out my hands, letting them tickle my palms and fingers. I could hear and feel them flapping all around me.

Their wings formed a luminous rainbow of colors. I instantly identified some black and gold monarchs, the butterflies that I'd loved watching as a child. This wasn't the kind of spirit guardian I expected, and I wasn't even sure what this meant. All I knew was that this gathering of butterflies made me feel supported, almost giddy. Almost like I could fly if I wanted to.

Just then, I heard the drumming increase its cadence. There was an urgency to the rhythm, and I knew I had to leave, despite wanting to remain in this colorful, almost surreal, land of butterflies. Ever so gently, I moved my arms and body to encourage the butterflies to take flight. Before stepping back into the tunnel, I felt an incredible sense of respect, love and regard for these tiny creatures who came to greet and protect me.

Getting through the narrow passage to the tunnel went quickly, and my return up the tunnel was effortless, kind of like being sucked into a gigantic vacuum cleaner. The drumming got faster and louder as I arrived at the tree trunk and crawled out of the opening. A few moments after that, I felt myself fully in my body again, and the drumming abruptly stopped. I could hear Jacki moving around me, from head to toe, with what sounded like a rattle.

"Let Traveler Ben keep his guardian close by as he learns to see like a Traveler."

When the rattling finally stopped, I was told to open my eyes. Traveler Jacki wanted to hear about my journey, and after sharing it, she seemed pleased to hear about the butterflies.

"Butterfly spirit means big, big change, Traveler Ben," emphasized Traveler Jacki, grabbing my attention. Her comment didn't surprise me, since the butterfly was a metaphor for resurrection and transformation. But I also knew that getting out of the cocoon or chrysalis unscathed was neither easy nor guaranteed. "What do you think of your guardian?"

"Well, I'm happy, even though the butterfly is not big and powerful. Say like the tiger, for example. I was kind of expecting to see a bigger, you know, more ferocious animal."

"Hey, Bear, look who wants to be a tiger." Jacki winked, and Bear howled and shook his head as if he was in full agreement.

"Oh yeah? Well look who wants to be a Bear," I said childishly, pointing at the spaniel, who proceeded to nuzzle and lick at my face. Jacki helped me to my feet, and what she said next was not comforting.

"Butterfly spirit is light, sweet and graceful. But it also has the power to transform. Now, you dance the dance of your spirit guide."

"You didn't say dance, did you? As in moving the body? This

body?"

"Yes! You must dance your spirit. How else can you come to know it?"

"That's true. I guess you're right. Besides, I always loved butterflies." After mustering up the courage, I clasped my hands under my chin and flapped my hands and arms up and down. It felt awkward at first, but soon my feet were dancing in a surprisingly quick and light way. They kept leaving the ground and propelling me upward. I even imagined I could feel the wind pushing me this way and that. Finally, my entire body got in to the act as Traveler Jacki picked up her flute and accompanied me. I must have danced for several minutes, until a flashlight shined on us from the hospital entrance.

"Who goes there?!" shouted a familiar voice. It was security guard Jeff.

I finished my dance as Jeff approached, one hand on his holster. When I waved and announced myself, Jeff let down his guard.

"What you doing out here, Doc Ben?"

"My friend, Jacki, was playing a song and…"

"Oh, hi, Jacki."

"Hi, Traveler Jeff."

"You two know each other?"

"Jacki's my bud. She made me this super bouquet of flowers. You know, for the wife. Went over big time," he said with a wink, adding a thumbs-up sign for good measure. Then, he looked at me. "So. Were you dancing or…?"

"Oh, right, that… I guess you could say that was kind of a dance. Not that you'd see anyone do it at a wedding."

"Sure hope not," grinned Jeff. "But hey, it's okay with me."

"Then you won't say anything?"

"Didn't see anything. Didn't hear anything. Carry on!" he smiled authoritatively, before turning and briskly walking back to his post.

Chapter 18

We'd been on the road for almost an hour, headed to the "place of deep waters," according to Traveler Jacki. She explained that she was guided here by the "Old Ones, the ancient Travelers." The car turned into a desolate parking area about thirty minutes southeast of Salem, the Oregon state capitol. This place of deep waters turned out to be only vaguely familiar to me.

Many years ago, I had come to Silver Falls State Park with Beth and Mel for a July fourth picnic. We didn't do much hiking because this park can fool you. It was known for its hiking trails and picturesque scenery. But in truth it was a wilderness spanning more than 9,000 acres, replete with 100-foot high waterfalls, caverns and cliffs. I didn't relish being out here at night.

"Can't we do this somewhere else? This could be dangerous."

"You gotta exercise your Traveler's eye in the wild for it to get strong."

"But it's almost midnight. We're not supposed to be in the park. No one's here."

"Then it ain't gonna be a problem."

"Yeah, but what if we see a park ranger?"

She gave me an irksome look before removing a flask from her backpack. She handed it to me. "This will help you see your guardians and keep you safe."

"How so? What is it? A hallucinogenic?"

"It's one-hundred percent natural. From herbs. Guaranteed to help you Travel."

"Traveler Jacki, are you sure? Is this really necessary?" I paused, holding the flask partway up to my lips.

"If you wanna be one, you gotta *see* like one."

"In that case... I'm open. I'm very open. Opening wide." I gulped down an earthen, foul-smelling brew that almost made me puke.

"Oh, one more thing. It might help if you squint."

"Squint?" Right then, I squinted until I could hardly see anything.

"Less, less. Just soften things. Like you're looking through sleepy eyes."

"How's this?" I squinted slightly while gazing softly at the surroundings.

"Better." She guided us to a trail inside the park. Traveler Jacki found a slender tree branch that was about four feet long and handed it to me. "Use this for walking. Or for fighting off animals." Then, she followed the trail at a very brisk pace.

"Animals? What animals? What if I lose you? Where do we meet?" I called loudly, but Jacki didn't answer, instead picking up the pace. "What animals?"

The sky clouded over, and the moon only intermittently peeked through. We passed a waterfall, and I heard the water crashing below me. I was just starting to think I would be okay until a wave of nausea overcame me. Vomiting made me feel better, but when I looked up, Jacki was quite a distance ahead. She alternately came in and out of view depending on the curve of the trail.

Finally, I couldn't see her at all. A feeling of panic clutched at my gut. I shouted her name, vainly trying to see into the darkness. Finally, I softened my gaze like she taught me, and that's when I saw Jacki waving at me far ahead. My relief was short-lived, though, when I discovered she had veered off on a less well-marked secondary trail.

"Damn." I broke into a jog so as to catch up. The trail was uneven, and my boot caught a downed tree limb and sent me reeling. My chin took the worst of it, and I felt a lot of blood on my face. From a sitting position, I pulled up my shirttail and held it on my chin to staunch the bleeding. When I finally stood up, there was no sign of Jacki, squinting or no squinting. My plan, which was the only plan I had, was to continue along this trail and meet her at the "deep waters" she had mentioned.

Unfortunately, the secondary trail was untended, and I tripped twice more, ripping my pants and scraping my knees and hands badly. My head was reeling, and I couldn't imagine making headway on this twisty, dangerous trail. That's when it occurred to me. Why not ask for help from my spirit guardian?

Now, you may not believe what happened next, and I'm not sure I believed it myself. But not a split second after I had that thought, a trail of luminescent butterflies materialized before me. Softening my gaze helped me see them stretched out in front of me, single file. I noticed that they followed the uneven terrain, thus letting me see where to step high over fallen branches, or when to move to either the right or left to avoid rocks and tree limbs.

With this visual aid, I was soon moving faster without fear of tripping or tumbling off the trail. I felt a renewed burst of energy and moved onward with alacrity, as well as possessing the odd sense that I was one with the trail. It was as if I knew what the terrain looked like around the next bend or hill before getting there. I never felt alone, but for my silent guides and the nearby hooting of an owl.

I must have gone on like this for an hour or more, for I had no way of telling time without my phone. Suddenly, the butterflies at the far front of the line came to a stop, bunching up to form what looked like a wall. I immediately slowed down and walked cautiously. All my senses became hyper alert, and I easily stepped over rocks and obstacles without consciously looking at them. In the distance, I heard the constant rush of water from a stream or a waterfall.

Several immense trees stood along the left side of the trail, while the right side hugged the edge of a steep hillside. Actually, it could have been a cliff because I couldn't make out anything very detailed, other than a drop-off into a dark void.

Then I felt it. The desperation. The focus. The need to kill.

Someone or something was staring at me. I even felt its fear and uncertainty. I don't know how I knew, but I was absolutely sure something meant to make a meal of me. Without moving my head, my eyes scanned the terrain until they moved upwards to a stand of firs about twenty feet away. My glance met the unyielding yellow eyes of a cougar. It was crouched on a fir tree branch, just a leap and two pounces from my warm neck.

It was not malicious, but the intent was there. I don't know which one of us blinked first. But I jumped off the trail as the cougar flexed its body midair. It all seemed to occur in slow motion as I tumbled down, scraping and bruising every part of my body on prickly brush, bumpy branches and rocky outcroppings. Desperately, I grabbed at everything in sight to slow my descent, but couldn't get a good handhold.

Just when I'd given up all hope, my body came to an abrupt halt, thanks to the remains of a dead tree stump. It hit me squarely in the chest, knocking the wind out of me. I waited in the darkness, trying not to move for fear of the cougar hearing me. But the truth was, I was so spent and exhausted that I think I passed out for a time.

When I came to, I could barely move and wondered if I'd broken a rib. Every inch of my body throbbed in pain. For a moment, the moon illuminated the landscape. That's when I discovered that the only thing between me and the edge of a cliff was this tree stump. Over the edge, I saw a pool of churning water far below. My battered condition made it impossible to climb back up. Besides, doing so would only provide a nicely tenderized meal for one hungry cougar. Sadly, I knew what this meant.

My only way out was down.

I called for help, which after a few tries, proved useless. Just when I was about to give up all hope, I heard the distinctive sound of powerfully flapping wings. A huge white snowy owl descended, landing not more than two feet uphill from me. Its face was pure white, with large golden eyes and a jet black beak. The long wings were white, with some brownish markings at the ends. I was stunned, but not afraid. When I squinted in disbelief, the owl's eyes narrowed like it was squinting back at me. Despite my pain and shock, I let out a short laugh. I didn't know what to think when the owl hopped around me, peering at me intently, as if assessing my situation.

Then, the majestic creature did something that I'll never understand. It scuttled across the ground until its imposing black talons were uncomfortably close to my neck. When its beak opened wide, I shut my eyes and grimaced, expecting the worst. I was stunned when the big owl clutched my jacket collar firmly in its beak and began flapping its mighty wings. I could feel myself being lifted up as the bird hovered more than three feet above the ground, helping me stand. Once I was stable and got my footing, it let go. It looked at me for a moment longer, then blinked at me with its piercing gold and black eyes before flying into the darkness.

I stood there for a minute or two, bent over and gasping in pain, wondering what to do next when an incongruous sound danced off the canyon walls. It was the sonorous music of a flute. Traveler Jacki's melodious song acted as a lone guide calling to me in the darkness.

Had she heard me calling? She must have. I shouted again,

but she just continued playing. Maybe she was simply letting me know where she was. Either way, my situation was dire. I almost dropped back onto the dusty ground when I saw what looked like a rope hanging in the sky. My guardians, not willing to let me go without a fight, were on a rescue mission. One of the butterflies near the end of the "rope" fluttered down beside my head. Right then, I heard a voice that wasn't my own.

Love is always given.

Funny what pops into your head when your life hangs by a thread. Why did I hear these words now? I knew there was love in the world, only I hadn't always given that love freely or unconditionally, which I knew was my own failing. But it occurred to me that my beloved Mel must have always known that. Hell, she lived it. Each day, even her last one, was precious, filled with love. I wondered, is that why she had no fear of death?

I dug into my pocket for the small metal tin that Katerina had given me. She said I'd know exactly when to open it up, and she was right. Incredibly, the tin was not bent in the slightest. I pried open the lid and found a small slip of paper, the kind you find in a fortune cookie. On it, written in Katerina's flowing script were the words, "Trust love, kiddo." I could only shake my head at this synchronicity. Several butterflies, adorned in multiple colors fluttered around and over the note, as if trying to read the latest and most important news.

I put the missive back inside the tin and snuggly fit it into a crevice on the tree stump. "Just in case another Traveler comes this way," I whispered aloud, as my spirit guardians formed the shape of a rope and wrapped themselves around my waist.

Normally, I feared heights. But jumping off a cliff, in the dark, above a raging waterfall? Freaking out seemed like a normal reaction, but instead I was calm, collected, aware of the littlest thing—each breath, my throbbing body, the radiant energy of every rock and tree. Suddenly, it occurred to me that I was more focused, present in action, engaged and alive than I'd been in years. The deep sense of wholeness that I experienced made me realize that this was how I wanted to live and love each moment. Senses wide open. Mind wide open. Heart wide open. Even if I had to die doing it.

That was my last thought as my body cleared the cliff.

Even before I started falling, I was enveloped in a cocoon formed by my butterfly guardians. The sensation of love, warmth and protection spread throughout my entire body. It was as if every cell of my being was supported and cared for. It wasn't so much of a thought as a feeling that came to me.

So this is what it feels like to live without fear and doubt and dread.

Just then, my body was jolted out of its protective cocoon by a powerful thud and abrupt immersion into a watery world filled with butterflies. A mesmerizing kaleidoscope of thousands of butterflies spun and twirled around me. Though I was trapped in the undercurrent of an immense and powerful washing machine, the butterflies wrapped around my wrists and tugged me in a lateral direction until finally, I was free. When I popped to the surface, I was amazed to find that Traveler Jacki was there, shouting for me to take hold of the long stick that she held out. I barely had enough strength to grab on as she pulled me to a shoreline of sand and rock.

We didn't speak. Traveler Jacki helped me hobble over to a fire she had started, and I sat down close to the flames. She looked serious as she took herbal medicine out of her backpack and rubbed it on my chin and hands. Meanwhile, Bear was happy to see me, licking my bruised hand. Jacki cradled my head as she tilted a bottle of water to my lips. I was so thirsty I drank the whole bottle without stopping for a breath. Traveler Jacki removed her jacket and wrapped it around my shivering body. She gave me some trail mix and we rested for a bit.

My head was still spinning as I asked, "What just happened back there? I saw things that... I don't understand how..."

Traveler Jacki picked up a thick, crooked branch. "Wood

already got the fire inside of it... wanting to be free, Traveler Ben," she said, tossing the branch into the flames and causing sparks and embers to fly into the air. "Just like we all got the light of the Traveler inside of us."

"Yeah, but why... why's it so hard to see?"

The flames flickered on Traveler Jacki's face, and I thought I saw a smile creep across her lips. "A big log, it don't catch fire on its own. Takes a lotta work, a lotta energy to turn even kindling into fire. For some, seeing their own light takes a whole lifetime... or more. Likes they say, it don't come easy, right, Bear?" Traveler Jacki glanced at Bear, who came over and rested his head on my thigh. When he moaned softly, as if commiserating with me, I couldn't suppress a smile. For the first time, I saw a subtle glow around Bear. Respectfully, I nodded back at this four-legged fellow Traveler.

After Traveler Jacki doused the fire, we picked up our things and trekked out. I glanced back at the pool, the waterfall and the cliff, which was a good fifty to sixty feet above the water. Part of me was horrified and could hardly believe that I survived. Another part of me was like, "Oh yeah, bring on the next cliff" — which was even more horrifying. We soon made our way to another trail that led to some steps as a welcome sign of civilization. In my exhausted state, I was pleased to discover that we were only minutes away from the park entrance.

On the drive back, my head cleared. When I told Jacki about how a white owl had checked on me and helped me stand, she didn't say a word. Still, I couldn't help but notice how the brown markings on the owl's wings matched those of the feather hanging from her hair. We arrived at the hospital just in time to see the sun rise in the reddish-tinged sky. I knew I needed a lot more time to absorb what had happened. One thing was for sure. As crazy as my nighttime journey had been, something in me had changed forever.

For perhaps the first time in my life, I had truly *seen*.

Chapter 19

The sound of someone yelling startled me awake. At first, I thought it was a dream, but then I realized there was an altercation happening nearby. It took a moment to get my bearings. Vaguely, I remembered wearily flopping myself down fully clothed on the cot in Traveler Jacki's cottage. Still groggy, I picked up my phone and blinked in disbelief. I couldn't believe it was almost a quarter to ten. I'd missed my first two morning appointments, which was a first for me. After looking around and seeing that I was alone, I stood, rather unsteadily, and went over to the window.

I watched as three police officers roughly removed someone from a police van. What shocked me was that the person shouting for help was Mason. He was handcuffed and had shackles around his ankles. I don't know why, but the first image that came to me was of a butterfly being held captive in a cocoon, not being allowed to fly free.

I dashed out of the cottage so quickly that I forgot my shoes. My eyes met Mason's, and he called to me for help. I could see the pure fear, almost oozing out of him like a greenish liquid, and it unnerved me.

"Sir, please stand back," ordered one of the policemen as he painfully twisted my arm and shoved me out of the way.

"I'm his doctor!"

"I seriously doubt that," chortled the officer, who looked at me dismissively, then blocked my access as Mason was brought to a side door. Fredo, one of our orderlies, held the door open.

"He's not cooperative, so we had to restrain him," explained one of the men carrying Mason.

"Fredo! Do not sedate him, whatever you do." I waved to make sure Fredo understood me.

"Sir, get on your hands and knees immediately." The cop turned to me, his pistol drawn.

"Officer, he's one of our doctors. That's Dr. Banks."

"Are you sure?"

"Oh yeah, that's him. What happened to you, Doc?"

"Bring him to my office. Fredo, you wait there with him." I entered the unit as Mason was moved inside.

The lead officer ignored me and spoke to Fredo. "Sorry. But we're supposed to bring him to a secure holding room."

"Well, I'm his psychiatrist, and I'm the one signing for his release."

Finally, the lead officer shrugged his shoulders. "Just so you know, you're responsible the second the restraints come off."

After they brought Mason to my office, I signed the paperwork, and they removed the restraints. I told Fredo to remain there while I cleaned up. I noticed Mason was breathing a little better, though eyes were swollen as if he'd not slept or had been crying. I reassuringly patted him on the shoulder.

"Mason, I'll come back and we'll get to the bottom of this."

"I fucked up. Big time."

"Don't worry. We'll figure it out."

"Dr. Banks? Did you get in a fight? You look like hell."

"That bad, huh? You just catch your breath and relax. I'll be back shortly."

Moments after leaving my office, I raced around a hallway corner and ran smack into Beverly, who was with Edward Delabrey. Seeing them together took me off guard, as I imagined my disheveled appearance did to them.

"Hello, Dr. Howell."

"Oh my God. What in the world? What happened to you?"

"Hello, Mr. Delabrey." I barely looked at him. "I uhm, I had a slight fall."

"Looks a hell of a lot worse than that. Get cleaned up, Dr. Banks. Then I want to see you in my office ASAP. It's about Mason."

Edward Delabrey puffed out his chest and sneered at me like I was a cockroach he was about to step on. When he gave a sideways glance to Beverly, I saw the faint outline of butterflies wrapping around the two of them, as if they were linked. It was subtle, but I could have sworn I saw something. I believe I may have squinted.

"Mason doesn't need restraints." I blurted out, to no one in particular.

"Oh really?" shot Delabrey, leaning aggressively toward me. "How the hell do you know what he needs? You call yourself a doctor? Look at you. Where are your shoes? You look like some kind of pathetic degenerate."

"Dr. Banks, where is Mason? I was sending him to forensics for observation."

"Forensics? Why?" I asked.

"Maybe if you checked your messages last night you'd know your patient got violent. There's an assault and a mental health commitment hold."

"Don't send him there, Beverly. I need to talk with him first. Please? I deserve that."

"Okay, Ben. But let me just say that your comportment here doesn't help your case. I'll see you later. We'll decide after."

Beverly and Delabrey walked past me, and I watched for a

moment as they entered Beverly's office. This surprised me, but maybe there were other issues about the mental health commitment that they were discussing. On my way out of the unit to get cleaned up, our receptionist, Fran, saw me.

"Dr. Banks, oh dear. Did we have a patient code?"

"Oh, God, no. But I kind of feel like it. I'm just going to clean up. Have you seen Jacki and her dog?"

She shook her head and held out a bandage she removed from her desk drawer. "Here, for your chin. You better give it a good cleaning first."

"Right and bright at ten, Traveler Ben!" I heard Traveler Jacki exclaim as she entered the waiting area. Instead of cleaning up, I escorted Jacki and Bear back to the unit. I made a short announcement to the patients about pet therapy, after which Jacki introduced herself and Bear to the group like an old pro.

"Holy shit, Bono," said Roy, who stood there, half-smiling and admiring my wounds. "Damn. Those groupies really roughed you up, huh?"

"Oh yeah, like you wouldn't believe," I winked. Roy fist-bumped me and pumped his arm up and down a couple of times.

I stepped back to watch Traveler Jacki and Bear interact with the patients. Bear had everyone's rapt and loving attention while Jacki stood off to the side, moving her hands all around, almost like a belly dancer. I wondered if she was somehow adjusting the energies and spirits of the patients.

From behind, an orderly tapped me on the shoulder. It was JoBee, the mental health tech. "Hey Buddy, you can't be out here with no shoes. You got no name tag. What room are you in?" he asked, looking at my rumpled appearance. "How's about we get you cleaned up?" He grabbed my arm and led me to the bathroom. When I saw myself in the mirror, I was shocked at how almost every inch of my body was scraped, swollen and bruised. My hair was crazy matted, my face unshaven. No wonder JoBee didn't recognize me. He handed me a fresh bar of soap.

"Thanks, JoBee. Maybe I'll just take this with me and get a shower."

JoBee finally looked directly at me, puzzled. "What the... Dr. Banks?"

"Thanks for the soap."

I felt a hundred times better after a quick shower. I returned to my office and put on a spare shirt that I kept there for emergencies. Then, Mason and I high-stepped it over to the unit in time to watch the end of pet therapy. Bear seemed to intuit what calmed and soothed patients. Depending on what was needed, he'd look into their eyes, sit quietly while being petted, or provide energy, running in circles and wagging his tail. All the while, Traveler Jacki wandered the perimeter, moving and dancing to unheard music. She only interceded if someone tried to get rough with Bear—not like he couldn't take care of himself.

I walked up and waved my arms. "Okay everyone, the pet visit is over for today. Bear needs to rest."

"This dog rocks!"

"Doc, can me and the dog go for a walk?"

"He looks just like BooBoo my pit bull. Come BooBoo, BooBoo come!"

I was happy to see patients energized in a positive way. Immediately, I noticed an increase in verbal and social interactions. Jacki encouraged Mason to pick up Bear. It was a beautiful moment when Bear licked Mason's face. Though Mason smiled only weakly, I was still happy to see it.

Jacki came over and whispered in my ear. "Kid's a natural."

"You can tell that just by looking at him?"

"He can help us find the treasure. I'm sure of it."

I looked around to make sure no one was nearby. "It's complicated. I can't just take him off the unit."

"We need him."

"We'll see."

The patients were still milling around Bear, so I asked how many persons liked the session. When almost all raised their hands, I announced that we'd schedule another pet session soon.

"Great show. Encore. Encore. Encore," exclaimed Roy, getting others to join in saying "encore" in unison. When Bear sat up on his haunches and barked as if on cue, the group burst into applause and laughter.

On our way to the exit, Traveler Jacki elbowed me in the side. "Don't forget. The treasure."

"Treasure?" said Mason.

"Oh, it's nothing. " I shrugged, much more concerned about Mason's immediate future than some ambiguous treasure. After thanking Traveler Jacki for her pet therapy group, Mason and I headed to my office. I could hardly wait to learn what had gone so wrong during his visit home.

Chapter 20

Instead of assuming his usual cross-legged position, Mason sagged over the arm of the sofa. Quickly, I phoned the nurses' station to reschedule my 11 am session. I needed to document the full extent of Mason's weekend before my meeting with Beverly.

"Okay, Mason, the decks are cleared." I swiveled my chair to face him. But before we could speak, we were jolted by a loud, high-pitched beeping sound coming from outside. I glanced out and saw workmen in orange vests setting up stanchions. I wondered if this was connected to the hospital expansion. When I turned my attention back to Mason, I found him to be low affect, struggling to tell his story.

As written in my chart notes:

The patient's affect is flat and his body limp. Patient is oriented to time and place, but makes very little eye contact. Patient's eyes are puffy, which patient states is from lack of sleep and crying while in police custody.

Patient constantly pulls at his hair, which is uncombed. When patient is questioned about compulsive hair pulling, he reports,

"Sometimes I pull my hair when I'm upset." Patient reports no history of pulling hair for long periods of time and has never had any hair loss from the behavior; As such, Trichotillomania, or hair pulling disorder, is ruled out.

Patient reports that the weekend had actually started off quite well. The patient's father was out of town on a business trip, so on Saturday, Mason stayed home with his sister, Dilly, and his mother. Patient reports they all went shopping in the afternoon, and that his mother bought him a new pair of shoes and shirts. They ordered his favorite pizza for dinner and watched TV that evening.

Mason had invited his friend Jodi for dinner on Saturday, but she was only able come over on Sunday. Patient reports that on Sunday, his older brother, Eddie Jr,. returned home in the morning from Oregon State University to pick up some belongings. The father returned about noon. Patient reports that at dinner that evening, *"Eddie was being a total asshole"* by constantly bragging to Jodi about being on the baseball team and acing his college classes. It was when Eddie rudely referred to Mason as *"mental"* that the patient left the dinner table without saying a word. Jodi followed him, and together they retreated to Mason's room.

Patient reports that Jodi helped calm him down when they were in his room. According to Mason, Jodi thought it was Eddie Jr. who was *"mental,"* and they actually laughed together. They were talking when there was a knock on the door of the room. Patient reports that he opened it and was confronted by Eddie Jr., who was brandishing a pellet gun that belonged to Mason. Eddie Jr. then said, *"If you were looking to show her your gun, don't bother. Dad gave it to me. He didn't think you could be trusted with one."*

The patient reports that what really enraged him was when his brother said to Jodi, *"If you want someone who knows how to use a gun, I'm the guy. I don't think Mason even knows what his 'gun' is."*

At this point in the story, Mason stopped and hung his head. I let him sit for a while. "Mason, are you all right? That must have felt very insulting and humiliating. Do you want to tell me what happened next?"

"I guess I exploded. If punching him in the face and fighting him for the gun counts as an explosion. We were on the floor fighting, and my father ran up the stairs and started kicking me. Jodi and my mother and Dilly were yelling for us to stop, but I must have snapped or something."

I said nothing, allowing Mason to process his experience. He buried his head in his arms, stifling any tears. Finally, he spoke, explaining what had happened.

"I got control of the gun, and I pointed it at my father and brother, and I threatened to shoot unless they got out of my way. I took Jodi's hand and we ran downstairs. I grabbed my dad's car keys off the counter on the way out."

As I looked at Mason, I felt an odd shift. It was subtle, but everything looked more vivid. My breath grew imperceptible, almost as if time itself had stopped. Out of nowhere, the image of a car rolling off a boat ramp and into the river flashed before my eyes. The image was so vivid, that I said aloud, "You didn't."

"Didn't what?"

"Uhm... I mean, you didn't take his car for a joy ride, did you?" I covered my tracks, thinking that the image in my mind's eye was just my imagination.

"I drove it to Clackamette park. We put it on the boat ramp."

"And..." I gulped.

"I dumped his precious Mercedes in the river. Did you know that the lights stay on underwater?"

"What happened to the gun?"

"Never fired it. Chucked it in the river."

"Were there pellets in that gun?"

"Don't know."

We sat for a long time in silence. My heart sunk. I didn't need to be psychic to know that attempted assault with a weapon or a pattern of psychotic behavior was enough reason to declare mental incompetency and have a guardian appointed. At the very least, a case could be made that for Mason's own welfare, as well as the welfare of those around him, that his mental illness posed an imminent threat. A win in court seemed unlikely, meaning he might remain in forensics for several months before another hearing. It could go on and on. But meanwhile, I feared irreparable damage would be done to the boy's esteem and future life options.

We spent some time trying to unpack the emotions that led to Mason's decompensating. I tried to normalize his feelings of humiliation. I even shared my feelings about his being kicked as a form of abuse. But Mason wasn't letting any of it seep in.

"Mason, I feel like you don't want to validate your reactions."

"Why should I? I fucked up and deserve to be locked up. Didn't you say that other people can't force you to feel a certain way? So if that's true, then my brother and father can be assholes, but it shouldn't bother me, right? I should be able to change my behavioral sequence, right? But I couldn't. I didn't change anything."

"There's no one simple way to view things, Mason. Isn't it also true that you left the dinner table without retaliating?"

"I suppose." He looked down at the floor.

"That's a behavior sequence change. You stood up to abuse from your brother and father, didn't you? You have every right to uphold your dignity. However, the gun was unfortunate."

"And the car." Mason sighed and finally looked up at me.

"Well, in retrospect, I'd rethink that one, too. But it must have felt damn good in the moment."

"My dad is gonna kill me for that. Especially now with the whole Attorney General election bullshit."

"What? Run that by me again."

"My dad's gonna rip me a new asshole."

"No, what you said about Attorney General?"

Mason proceeded to tell me that his father had proudly

announced to the family that he was being endorsed to run for the office of Oregon Attorney General. I rarely paid attention to the news, and I asked if this was general knowledge. Mason said that there was going to be a press conference to announce it, and that was all he knew.

"So, what happens now?" Mason's fearful expression told me he needed some hope. All I had was a dose of reality.

"I'm going to do my best to keep you on this unit. But I think your father will push for long-term treatment."

"Long-term?"

"It's where the people with chronic and acute mental illness stay. It's called the forensic unit, which is another wing of our hospital. One last thing, Mason. Did you see the Traveler? It's okay if you did. I just need to ask."

"Yeah, just briefly."

"Really? When?"

"Last night, in a holding cell at the Clackamas police station."

"What did he say?"

"Call Dr. Banks."

My first thought upon hearing that was "Oh shit," because I didn't want to document any auditory hallucinations in my chart notes. But given my past omissions, I had no choice but to include it.

"Mason, are you sure about that? Maybe it was just your own thoughts?"

"No, it was the Traveler. I closed my eyes and saw him. He leaned forward and whispered that to me. That's why I called you Sunday night from the jail. Didn't you get my call?"

I apologized profusely for being indisposed, before glancing at the clock and realizing it was noon. I walked with Mason to the lunchroom, letting him know I'd check in with him later.

In my office, I quickly composed my chart notes, which unfortunately included mention of an auditory hallucination. My notes concluded that Mason's behavior, while not condoned, was understandable given that he was both threatened and physically confronted. Further, there was a recommendation to increase the patient's current dose of olanzapine from 5 mg to 10 mg. Finally, hoping to keep Mason in my unit, I wrote under the Plan section of my SOAP note that more observation was needed before determining a diagnosis of schizophrenia.

Out of nowhere, an image of Beth burst into my mind. I felt truly horrible about not informing her of my whereabouts the previous night. I'd frequently thought of calling her, and now that I had a moment, I called her office. Sadly, she was gone, and so I left a short voice message. I was particularly concerned that my absence after our recent talk would send the wrong message.

I decided it would do me good to go outside for a breath of fresh air to clear my head. That's when I spied a sign standing near the stanchions that had blocked off much of the front grounds. The sign read: *We're Growing with a New Treatment Clinic.*

They sure weren't wasting any time to get this new clinic built. As I followed the perimeter of yellow tape printed with the words *No Trespassing*, I thought I heard someone calling.

"Benjamin, where have you been?" I swiveled around to see Beth marching toward me. A powder blue purse swung from her shoulder. "I didn't hear a peep from you. I've called and texted!"

"I'm so sorry. I meant to call, but…"

"I know I talked about separating, but I never said anything about disappearing! Damn you!" She saw the bandage and other marks and bruises on my face. "My God. Were you in an accident? What happened?"

"A minor… accident. I'm okay, really. It's just, well, there've been some developments."

"An accident? You've always called if... if you weren't coming home. It's not fair of you to do that! You can't just disappear on me and have an accident!"

Beth blinked back tears. She angrily flailed her hands at me, not really meaning to hit their target. I pulled her close.

"Something's happening that I don't really understand. You have to trust me, Beth. I didn't mean to stay away or not call. But I went on a sudden... I don't know what to call it. An *impromptu journey.*"

"Impromptu journey?"

"Yeah, with, uhm... with our new gardener." I pointed over to Traveler Jacki, who was trimming tree branches by the fence. "It meant nothing. Well actually, it did mean something."

"*Impromptu journey.* Oh, so that's what they call an affair now?" she said, breaking away from me.

"No, no. It's not that. Not an affair. She's teaching me. She's a, uhm, I don't know... she calls herself a Traveler, okay?"

"Oh? Like an escort? No, please, don't tell me. I came here because I still have feelings for you, Ben. Although I'm not sure why."

"You do? You still have feelings for me?"

"Yeah, what do you think? I worry about you, you crazy old bastard. But now, with your *impromptu journey* or whatever, I need more time to think," she said, her abrupt turn stalled as I grabbed her arm and kissed her. We looked at one another for a long time. I squinted, but didn't see anything around her.

"Why are you squinting?"

"I'm not squinting."

"You're squinting."

"Look, Beth, I can't explain it to you right now. But things are different."

"Must have been one hell of an 'impromptu journey.'"

"Will you please stop saying that? It wasn't what you... Look, can we talk about it at dinner? Tonight?"

"I don't know."

"Six. We'll make dinner together."

"Things still have to change, Ben. Really change." She stood there for the longest time, shaking her head with an expression of exasperation. "I'm not giving up Judge Judy without a fight."

Chapter 21

That afternoon I tried to see Dr. Howell at her office, but that meeting never materialized. Given my untimely meeting with Beverly and Edward Delabrey in the hallway earlier, I feared my position was tenuous. Worse, any discussion would now occur in front of the staff.

Beverly began the staff meeting on a cheerful enough note, declaring that financing for the new expansion had just been finalized. We would soon house a state-of-the-art eating disorder clinic for adults. The centerpiece of the program would be Cognitive Processing Therapy (CPT), along with Equine Therapy (ET) in association with a nearby equine facility that stabled over fifteen Arabian horses. But her upbeat tone quickly grew severe.

"There's never a good time to announce bad news. But the fact is, there's been a serious breach of the standard of care at this institution. We require that our formal Mental Status Examination be completed during the initial intake, and updated as needed. Someone here has not met that standard." She turned her gaze slowly in my direction. "Dr. Banks?"

I tried to sit up as straight as possible. "Okay, uhm, okay... I may have not used the exact Mental Status Exam template. But it's all there, in my notes... informally. I want to establish the therapeutic alliance first and then..."

"That's not good enough, doctor. I will not have this organization jeopardized because of lackadaisical work."

I quickly glanced around the room, and everyone's eyes were peeled on me with expressions of skepticism and apprehension. Let's put it this way. If this was a courtroom and my colleagues were the jury, I'd have gone for the plea bargain. Even the normally smirking Dr. Rick viewed me askance, as if I'd been convicted of some awful, grizzly crime.

Beverly leaned forward in a predatory posture. "Since we're discussing standards, I learned from Mason Delabrey's parents that he mentioned having multiple hallucinations. And yet, these are also conspicuously absent from your notes."

I wriggled uncomfortably in my chair, like I was sitting before a prosecutor and not a colleague. "I documented the last one, so..."

"Yes, the last one. Thank you for mentioning that," she said, positioning her laptop in front of her. "I have your electronic records here. And you write, 'The patient reports seeing the image of a man who then whispered to him, "Call Dr. Banks."' Oh, so you're actually part of the patient's psychosis now, is that correct?" Beverly impatiently tapped her fingers on the desktop.

"But in the proper context, he's made progress that..."

"Progress?..." she interrupted, just beneath the threshold of anger. "Do you call it progress when someone goes home and violently holds his family at gunpoint, and then dangerously drives a car into the river?"

I could feel my own anger threshold rising. "But if Edward Delabrey kicked his son, then maybe we need to mandatory report the incident to Adult Protective Services."

"You're going to indict a man who was protecting his family

from a violent act? I've heard quite enough. That is not abuse. In truth, Edward Delabrey has done more for this hospital and our upcoming expansion..." Beverly paused, as if she had said too much. She closed her laptop in a very controlled and composed way. "Dr. Banks, I have no choice but to report you to the licensing board. You can remain working pending your board's investigation. But any future notes will be read and double-checked by others. Is that clear?"

After a long silence, I felt I had to speak up. "You all know I would never put anyone at risk. And I'm very, very sorry for what happened."

Beverly looked directly at me. "One more thing. Mason Delabrey has been officially transferred to forensics. I've assigned him to Dr. Trent."

"But... I thought we were going to talk about this."

"There's now a felony assault charge signed by his entire family. There's no judge in the world who wouldn't want this young man to get the help he deserves."

"Can I at least see him? It would help Mason adjust to..."

"No, Ben. It's clear you've blurred your professional boundaries. Okay, then. Let's move on." Her voice softened, but not the message.

For the remainder of the meeting, I sat there like a hollow shell. I didn't contribute anything to the other case evaluations. All I could think about was how to help Mason, to speak with him and keep him off heavy-duty antipsychotic meds. Problem was, I couldn't muster a single useful idea.

I imagined a vulture-type energy perched atop Beverly's head, waiting to pick over me as it would an injured carcass. But no matter how much I squinted, I saw nothing. Whatever Traveler's second sight I possessed the previous night had evaporated. When the meeting ended, I left the room feeling very alone. Not even a single person said goodbye or came within arm's length of me.

Chapter 22

Over the next few days, I found it difficult to concentrate. I wasn't really present with my patients, either. And my dinner that evening with Beth, which I hoped would benefit us, threatened to further damage our relationship. When I disclosed that I had been put on report with my licensing board, Beth responded with shock. She calmed down when I explained that I'd keep working, but would need supervision for a period of time. Still, she insisted that my obsession with helping Mason was not normal, and that I needed to move on.

It helped that I decided to be upfront with Beth about my visits and trainings with Traveler Jacki, who I described as being a kind of healer or shaman. We sat in Mel's Shrine as I described my *journey*, from my initial inner excursion to find my guides to my midnight sojourn with the cougar, the cliff, and the falls. Initially, she was alarmed by my story and wondered if I wasn't having a breakdown of some kind. I couldn't have blamed her for thinking this. But when Beth saw how comfortable I was being with her in Mel's old room, she had a change of heart. Whereas before, I would have been bitter and demanded that the shrine was unhealthy and had to go, that was no longer the case.

In fact, Beth was quite moved when she heard how I sensed Mel's presence, or should I say her love. That same evening, Beth divulged her experiences with prayer, which I likewise found affirming. It was the first time we had shared these types of experiences. All told, I sensed a softening in each of us, and what had once pulled us apart was starting to bring us together. Or so I hoped.

Around that same time, unbeknownst to Beth, I put together a list of the friends I'd stopped communicating with over the past year. One by one—difficult conversation by difficult conversation—I reached out. Although the calls were painfully awkward, I couldn't help but notice one salient change. Instead of being overwhelmed by emptiness and bitterness after learning about their children, I felt happy for my friends. Were there times when, after hanging up the phone, that my tender heart grew sadder? Yes, but it didn't close up. Progress, right?

Another odd thing. I'm not sure why, but I began noticing my own mental tendency to either grab onto an idea I liked or to avoid one that was unpleasant. I even found myself pausing and grinning at things like a silly little kid. I mean, everything looked shiny and new—little things beautiful things, ugly things, even things that didn't make sense. My more laissez-faire way of being meant, for example, that I no longer had to make Mel's Shrine a point of contention. The whole effect was liberating, like taking off a pair of mental handcuffs. That said, I wasn't sure if it would last. Besides, I was not yet ready to fully embrace what was fundamentally the antithesis of my normal patterns of thinking, reacting, self-identity and awareness.

While Beth was connecting with this more laid-back version of me, it didn't help my case that each evening I waited until dark before driving back to the hospital to secretly train with Traveler Jacki and Bear.

Most nights, Traveler Jacki led me on journey into the spirit world where I reconnected with my butterfly spirit guides. This was supposed to strengthen my contact with them so I could reach them whenever needed. Afterwards, we walked around the grounds to scan various areas for the treasure. Traveler Jacki was vague whenever I asked for details about the treasure. But I'd grown to trust her intuition.

The procedure was simple. I rang a small bell that was supposed to call the ancient spirits. I was surprised at how the high-pitched sound seemed to heighten my senses. Meanwhile, Traveler Jacki raised the green-gold crystal high above her head. She instructed me to follow behind, looking for anything unusual, although I hadn't the faintest idea what that could possibly be. One difficulty was that several construction trucks had been moved into place and were blocking our way. We snaked around excavators, graders, and dump trucks. It was taking forever. That's when I turned to Jacki.

"Hold on about ten minutes. I have a surprise."

"Where you going?"

At the entrance, I found security guard Jeff nodding off in a chair. I knocked on the door and he startled awake.

"Sorry to bother you, Jeff."

"Hey, Doc Ben. What-up?"

"Forgot something in my office. Journal reading for the weekend."

"Sure." He punched in the night alarm code. "Hey, what have you and Jacki been doing out there?"

"Oh, yeah. It's a uhm... a blessing ceremony that she says will help the construction crew. You know, keep everyone safe."

"You just do your thing. It's dark, so be careful."

"Jeff, you wouldn't mind leaving that alarm off for an hour or so? I may need to come in and out a couple of times."

Jeff shot me a thumbs-up sign and settled back in his chair.

In the hallway, I could hardly believe my eyes and blinked

just to be sure. A subtle line of luminescent butterflies appeared before me, just as they had when I was on the darkened trail. I followed them around a corner to where they stopped at the bottom of a door. Approaching closer, I realized this was Dr. Howell's office. The administrative hallway had no cameras, and I tried turning the doorknob, but with no success.

Why had my spirit guides led me here? I heard a noise, and my heart started pounding loudly. I swiftly went to my office and sat down to collect myself. It was an old building and the door locks were easily hacked. I remembered how I had once used two paperclips to gain entry to my own office. It was a silly trick that I learned in college. So much for the value of an undergraduate degree.

Still, I couldn't shake the feeling there was something in Beverly's office that I needed to see. I fished two paper clips from my desk drawer. Then, I called Bob Trent, my friend on the forensic unit. I'd spoken with Bob previously, and he agreed to let me "borrow" Mason from his unit anytime I wanted, but on one condition: Only once, and only for 30 minutes. Bob would walk Mason to my office, and wait for me to return Mason a half hour later. I had some misgivings about my plan, and I took a deep breath.

"Bob, this is Ben. Can you escort Mason to my office in 10 minutes? Okay, great."

Hiding the paper clips in the palm of my hand, I approached Beverly's door. My fingers fumbled with the clips. Then, I took a breath and imagined I was back in college, hacking into my friend Travis Sunshine's dorm room. Suddenly, I felt the top clip catch and move. I pulled it steadily until the latch released. In the room, I turned on the lights, then instantly turned them off. What if someone from the hallway noticed that the lights were on? No, I reasoned, no one would notice, and besides, I needed the lights.

Nothing on Beverly's desk was out of the ordinary. Then I

saw a file cabinet with the label *Hospital Expansion*. Inside, there were a lot of design plans and estimates for work. The one folder that caught my eye simply read *Funding*. I flipped through to see the list of loans and finances for the new expansion until I saw the name Edward Delabrey. He had just contributed a major donation of over six figures. Suddenly, Beverly's insistence on putting Mason in forensics made sense.

Was this a subversive attempt to keep Mason quiet and out of the way during Edward Delabrey's political run for Attorney General?

Using my phone, I took several photos showing the date and time of his donation. Not coincidentally, that major donation was made the exact same day that Mason was returned to the hospital in restraints. And probably just moments after I'd seen Dr. Howell and Delabrey come into this office.

When I turned to go, I accidentally bumped into a large brown bin with the label "To Be Shredded." That's when I spied my stapled Sasquatch report atop the jumble of papers. Given everything else I had just learned, it didn't shock me. All I could do was to ruefully shake my head.

When I left, I made sure to re-lock the latch. I had no idea how long I'd been snooping around, but the timing was perfect. As I reached my office, Bob and Mason approached from the other direction.

"Thirty minutes, not a second more," warned Bob.

"Got it." I nodded at Bob and grabbed Mason by the arm.

"Dr. Banks, where're we going?"

"Outside. Just follow me." When we reached the waiting area, I saw that Jeff had nodded off again. We crept around him and were soon outside relishing the brisk night air.

When Traveler Jacki saw us, she ran up to Mason and gave him a big hug. Mason brightened when Bear jumped up to get some attention.

"We only have 30 minutes. Should we start looking?"

"Not so fast, you silly Traveler. We got to remove the dragons from this boy."

Mason defensively put up his hand. "Whoa. You're gonna do what?"

Traveler Jacki explained that the two dragons Mason had drawn were, in reality, harmful spirits that were attached to him. They were sucking away his life energy and filling him with poisonous venom of confusion and anger. Traveler Jacki turned to face Mason.

"Do you want me to remove them?"

"Hell yeah," he answered without hesitation.

Reaching into her backpack, she pulled out a hand drum for herself and a rattle for me. After handing over the rattle, she gave me a stern warning. "Traveler Ben, you just do what I say. Don't try doing this, because when you remove harmful spirits you can poison yourself if you're not careful."

We walked to an open clearing away from the machinery. The journey was done under the sky and the stars, which were exceedingly bright. With Mason lying on the ground, I circled him with a protective chant that Traveler Jacki told me to sing. My job was to shake the rattle at a constant rate, as a way to help amplify the protective field around him.

As I understood it, this protective field was twofold. First, it kept out any intrusive spirits that might try to enter during the vulnerable period. Secondly, it acted as a barrier that kept the dragon spirits from escaping should they somehow get past Traveler Jacki, who was, in her own words, "gonna suck these bad boys out and lock 'em away."

Before we started, I asked Traveler Jacki to explain where hostile spirits came from and why they attacked people. She said hateful spirits spread like any nasty disease when conditions were right. Once a hurtful spirit afflicted the mind, it also afflicted the body. I smiled to myself when hearing this explanation, because it was very much what research studies had learned about how both unhappiness and happiness spread among social groups, just like a virus.

When we started, I circled Mason for several minutes as Traveler Jacki loudly beat the hand drum. She moved ever closer to Mason's torso, all the while appearing to dodge an unseen enemy. Then, after some powerful shouts, she started to sing. As best I can remember, she repeated these verses several times:

Dragon, dragon,
grow feeble and weak.
Dragon, dragon,
fall deep to sleep.

Travelers, travelers,
both far and near.
Release these spirits
of pain and fear.

Jacki motioned for me to pick up the tempo. It was almost like a fever pitch when she knelt down beside Mason and bent over his abdomen. There was a loud sound as Jacki sucked the hostile spirits out of the young man's stomach. I winced as she leaned over and spit a huge slimy black glob from her mouth into a reddish clay pot on the ground next to her.

I continued my rattling as Jacki again leaned over Mason's gut, producing a prodigious sucking sound. She gasped and coughed, but then continued sucking. I stood directly beside Traveler Jacki to get a closer look as she opened her mouth and for several seconds vomited the most grotesque and vile snake-like mass into the container.

Traveler Jacki swiftly pressed a lid securely onto the clay pot. After resting for a few moments and taking some deep breaths, she signaled for me to slowly stop my protective vibrations. We checked in on Mason, and he answered weakly when asked how he was feeling.

Dr. Bob had wisely titrated Mason off his existing medications before adding an antipsychotic. But it seemed that this spirit removal had done something to him. Already, I noticed that his normally pale face started to show some color. He gazed up at us with a serene and peaceful expression, inhaling and exhaling deeply, almost as if a great weight had been removed from his shoulders.

When I asked how he was feeling, Mason had a bewildered expression, before saying that he felt "different, lighter, stronger." He paused for a beat before smirking, "Sorry, Dr. Banks, I know those aren't on the feelings chart."

"You got me there," I smiled, convinced that an emotional blockage in Mason had budged. "Now we can find the treasure?" I looked at the time on my phone, worried that we had almost used up our half-hour allotment.

"No, silly. He still needs a protective guide. Like your butterflies."

"Butterflies?" said Mason, attempting a wan smile.

I nodded seriously. "You'd be surprised. Butterflies can be very potent."

Mason was told to lie down with his head pointed to the North. Then we did a spirit guide journey for Mason, which was similar to mine only in terms of the basic steps. Mason's experience was totally unique. He described visiting an upside down land where the ground was above and the sky below. It was there that he connected to his guide, Eagle.

Eagle, as I had always understood it, was a symbol of courage and perspective. The eagle attained heights from which deeper truths could be found and spoken. For native traditions, Eagle spirit was sacred, a bringer of sacred wisdom. I didn't say any of this to Mason, but just waited for him to sit up and tell us about his encounter.

Mason, however, was not yet buying into his newfound spirit. "I dunno. What if all this was just, you know, my imagination."

"I thought the same thing at first," I added with a shrug.

Jacki lifted up the clay container in which she'd spit up the dragons. "Go, on. Have a look." She handed the jar to Mason, who timorously accepted.

Mason gripped the lid, which was held tightly. He twisted it back and forth until it released. A slimy, snarling two-headed snake with fearsome fangs appeared. Just as it looked to strike, Mason slammed down the lid. He looked at the jar, aghast, eyes wide open.

"Holy shit. What the fuck was that?" He shoved the container back into Jacki's hands.

"I don't understand it, either, Mason. Most people can't see it."

"That's your answer? I thought you were a doctor."

"It's like when the Traveler took you out of your body. Same thing."

"No, no, no. This is *much* weirder shit."

"We need your help finding the Treasure," affirmed Jacki as Mason stood up.

"Uhm, okay… but I don't know what to do."

"Use your spirit guide, not your eyes. Let Eagle show you the way." Jacki placed her hands upon Mason's shoulders and nudged him forward. Eyes closed, he started walking around the grounds. We followed him past a *No Trespassing* sign to an open grassy area near a bulldozer.

"Wow, yeah, something's happening," said Mason, who then turned in a different direction.

"What?" I asked.

"I think I'm seeing my Eagle guide high above, and it's showing me a dim glow nearby."

"Squint," I added, feeling like a wise elder.

"Uh-uh. He don't need to do that." Traveler Jacki shook her head at me.

Mason raised his arms in front of him, palms down. He

moved this way and that, like a basset hound following a scent. Finally, he was locked in. He crouched down and reached out with his hand.

"Here," he said, patting the ground several times before opening his eyes. "It's glowing. Right here."

A vibration in my pocket startled me. My phone was blowing up with messages from Bob. It had been an hour since Bob put Mason in my trusted care. "I have to get Mason back inside. Mark the spot, and we'll dig another time, okay?" Traveler Jacki nodded and marked the location with some twigs.

Thankfully, security officer Jeff was snoring, despite all the noise we made. When we reached Bob's office, he was frowning, arms akimbo.

"Thirty minutes, huh?" deadpanned Bob.

"Have a good weekend, O' great one." I spread my arms wide and made a grand bowing motion. This was my way of letting him know that I owed him big time, and we both knew it. A few minutes later, Bob texted that no nurses were at the station when he brought Mason back inside.

I couldn't help but wonder how the healing Traveler Jacki had done with Mason would pan out. While I was optimistic, I feared that things could get a lot worse if he remained in forensics.

Chapter 23

Over the weekend, I pondered how to best handle the information I'd gleaned in Beverly's office. Things got complicated when I turned on the local television news, only to witness Edward Delabrey announcing his candidacy for Attorney General. Wearing an elegant navy blue suit and seated on a plush leather chair, Edward was dutifully surrounded by his very loving, adoring, and also impeccably dressed family of Eddie Jr., Dilly and Shirley. When explaining what he stood for, he stressed family values and made the point that he was against guns and gun violence.

Conveniently, Delabrey had failed to mention, as Mason had told me, that he'd purchased pellet guns and rifles for both sons before they reached high school age. Or that he had another son whom he had conveniently removed from the family. After viewing this, I wanted to shout out the truth to Beth, or anyone. But I was bound by professional ethics to uphold patient confidentiality and the Health Insurance Portability and Accountability Act, known as HIPAA. I couldn't share a shred of this with a news outlet. Delabrey was a liar who, in my opinion, had committed his own son in order to make himself look like the perfect family man. Unfortunately, he was protected by the law and knew it. While I had no idea how, I realized that I'd have to accelerate my actions to protect Mason.

Back at work on Monday, the first thing I did was visit forensics. My plan was to assess Mason and find out what meds he was on.

"Baba want the fornication meadow landing cup," mumbled a floridly psychotic patient walking nearby. "Gucci peach baritone lettuce fandango?" she asked me with a very serious and intent expression.

"Oh yes, absolutely. I'd like two of those, please." I smiled and moved toward the television area. It never ceased to amaze me what some patients were capable of verbalizing, while acting as if their word salad made perfect sense.

When I noticed Sasquatch lumbering ahead, I stopped and tried to see if I could sense if anything was attached to him. Even squinting, nothing appeared, maybe because I was too focused on completing my other mission. Scanning the patient area, I saw Mason lounging languidly on a chair in the television room. Although a cartoon blared in the background, his heavily lidded eyes stared blankly ahead. He wasn't wearing his own clothing anymore, but the loose-fitting gowns that had no ties in an attempt to minimize ligature risk.

If you inspected the unit, you'd find that there was almost nothing that could be used as a ligature point from which a rope or bedspread could be attached in order for a patient to attempt suicide. All the surfaces were rounded, the utensils bendable plastic, and even the hinges and door handles were designed as non-weight bearing. Reducing ligature risk was understandable, but as a result, the environment was extremely gloomy and disheartening.

I pulled up a chair. "Hey, Mason. How's it going?"

"I dunno," he slurred, barely moving his head to look at me. After a few unsuccessful attempts to engage him, I reached over and gave his shoulder a squeeze of support. I wondered if Shirley had seen her son in this condition. I was upset and angry this had happened, and would call her later despite my no longer being Mason's therapist.

I stood around, pretending to review a patient folder, until I spied a nurse, Sandra, pushing a medication cart. She was an old-timer back from my time on the unit who I liked and trusted. Even though I no longer had electronic access to Mason's records, I explained to her that I had worked with him. "No problem," she said, handing over his chart. I saw that he was being given both a sedative and the antipsychotic drug Risperdal.

Drugs like Risperdal reduced psychotic symptoms by blocking dopamine receptors in the brain. According to the prevailing medical viewpoint, dopamine was implicated in motivation, excitement, interest in one's surroundings, and even coordination. An excess of it in the brain was linked not only to psychosis, but also to increased risk-taking and even addiction. Such issues, however, were not relevant to Mason. While muting excess dopamine might be helpful for some, in Mason's case it posed the risk of diminishing curiosity, engagement in life and his ability to see the Traveler.

I left forensics feeling extremely troubled, and I knew that I couldn't let Mason be exiled to what was a prison for his body and his soul. In fact, I vowed I wouldn't. Now, that might not sound like a psychiatrist talking, but seeing him in an almost vegetative state stirred me to action. Any shred of laissez-faire attitude I had possessed earlier was gone, replaced now by an all-consuming, laser-like resolve and urgency.

The first thing I did was call Shirley Delabrey. Since I was no longer Mason's care provider, I used my personal phone and got right to the point.

"Hello, Shirley, this is Dr. Banks."

"Oh." She sounded stunned. "Sorry, I can't talk now."

"Please, Shirley. It's important. Have you seen Mason since he was transferred to the long-term unit at the hospital?"

"I thought you weren't his doctor anymore. What's wrong?"

"I'm not. But I just saw Mason, and I'd like you to go see him for yourself."

"Why? Isn't he being cared for?"

"You need to go because you're his mother, and he needs you." There was a long silence on the phone.

"Edward told me stay away during the campaign."

"Oh? Remember your family history, Shirley."

"Sorry, I have to go."

"You have my direct line. Call me anytime, okay?" I felt that Shirley could shift the balance in Mason's favor, but only if she got involved.

A few moments later, I set in motion part two of my plan. Although I had knocked unannounced, the door to Dr. Howell's office creaked open. I figured having the element of surprise was a good thing, and so I walked right in. Her desk was littered with papers and plans.

"Oh, Ben, come in. I was just going to call you."

"Good, because I wanted to talk with you, too." Beverly took a seat behind her desk, and I sat down opposite. My breath was shallow and my hands clammy, but before I could make my accusation, she piped up.

"We're starting construction today. Exciting, isn't it?"

"I didn't know."

"Hmmmn. Really? I thought you would, since you broke into my office on Friday night."

This caught me off guard, and I felt my heart thumping. How did she know?

"See that?" She pointed up at a corner of the room. "It's a

video camera. I had it installed about a year ago."

"I don't have anything to hide, Beverly. But you do. I found about you and Edward Delabrey." I half stood and swiped at my phone, trying to find my photos. "He gave you money for the expansion, didn't he? In exchange for keeping his son out of the way during the election."

"You've got to be kidding me." She confidently picked up her desk phone and dialed the receptionist. "Fran, this is Dr. Howell. Is the security officer there? Good. Send him to my office immediately. Thanks."

I held up the phone for her to see. "See? Dated the same day Mason came back. That's over $100,000.00 dollars he gave you."

"Dr. Banks, take a chill pill. Don't you recognize what a wonderful gift this is for the mental health community? It's going to be featured in our newsletter." From her desk, she picked up a newsletter with a headline that had the words "Philanthropist Delabrey" and "the New Expansion."

"Huh? I don't get it?"

Beverly explained that it was common for parents to contribute money to the hospital where their loved ones were staying. She handed me several other pages with contributions. Some were even for amounts in excess of what Delabrey had given. At some point, while I was reviewing the donations, officer Jeff arrived and stood by the open door.

"For his generosity, Edward Delabrey will get his name engraved on one of the bricks outside the new treatment center. In fact, we will soon be buying up two more hospitals for our medical group. And, as the one who drove the fundraising campaign and did the planning, the Board has agreed to name me as their next President."

I was stunned, trying to absorb what the hell had just happened. My confidence was deflated, and I felt like crawling under the desk. How had I so terribly misread the situation?

"But you, Dr. Banks, will not be joining the glorious future of this organization. Did you really think I wanted *you* to be Executive Director?" Beverly snickered under her breath. "Your breaking in here made it easy for me. You are terminated immediately for unauthorized entry and theft of company information. Just to be clear, I've already reported the theft to your licensing board. Jeff, will you please escort Dr. Banks to his office to collect his belongings. Then see him off the grounds."

I stood, dazed and numb. I half-stumbled out of the office, feeling like a sledgehammer had just knocked me senseless. Jeff was upset, biting his lip and looking away. More than once, he blurted out that he was just doing his job.

Like a robot, I stacked my books and personal knick-knacks into two cardboard boxes that Jeff had found. I picked up the Rubik's Cube sitting on my desk and pondered it for a moment. Just like the puzzle of events encircling me now, I could never solve this damn cube. I wanted to throw it out, but instead, carefully placed it in the box.

I'd spent much of my professional life at the hospital, and to have it end so abruptly was shattering. I felt like I'd been gut-punched in the solar plexus. After everything was packed, Jeff rolled in a hand truck and loaded it up. I could feel my body trembling as I stepped down the hall. What would people think? How would I ever hope to work again? Worst of all, what about Mason, whom I had failed miserably?

Entering the lobby behind Jeff, my eyes locked onto Fran. A startled expression spread over her face. I paused at her desk.

"Goodbye, Fran. It's been great knowing you."

Fran jumped up and hugged me hard, her red curls covering my shoulder. When she let go, her eyes were teary. "Will you come back?"

I just shook my head. Outside, it had started raining, and little divots of water filled up holes on the grass around where the stanchions had been placed. I could sense every minute sprinkle that nipped at my face. Officer Jeff was kind enough to maneuver the hand truck out to my car.

The grinding sound of machinery exploded in my ears as construction was underway. After loading my trunk with the boxes, I shook Jeff's hand.

"Been good, Doc Ben. Real good."

"Same here, Jeff. You take care." We both leaned forward and gave ourselves a much-needed man hug.

"Sorry to see you go." He waved as he retreated, the hand truck trundling behind him. Before I drove off, I took one last look back at what might have been.

Too bad I'd never get to be part of it.

Chapter 24

I was too ashamed and embarrassed to tell Beth what had happened, so I left the next morning as if I was headed off to work, but really, I set up shop at the library. Instead of choosing the local West Linn Library, I opted for the Oregon City Library where I was less likely to run into someone I knew. It was a short drive over an old, narrow concrete bridge, from which I could see Willamette Falls. The library was a modernized old landmark that from one angle showed off a tastefully sculpted red brick edifice. From the other side, it featured an open, reflective structure with large panes of glass. Inside, the space offered several nooks and areas perfect for researching in private.

For the next few days, I situated myself on the second-floor corner of the building. Outside, I could see an expanse of green space dotted with benches and several large maple trees, as well as the sprawling beige building and longtime home of Clackamas County Fire Department, Station 15. An old neon sign reading *FIRE DEPT* in bright orange letters was mounted over the garage doors.

I'd never felt so low, so adrift. Rather than ruminate on

the dreaded visit with my licensing board, I decided to keep myself occupied. What better distraction than diving into the rabbit hole of alternate realities, of which there was no dearth of information. Spirits and illusion, for example, were woven into all the ancient native traditions and modern religions. Entities like sprites, elves, yetis, faeries, the Loch Ness Monster, angels and aliens were embedded in folklore and literature for eons. But were these entities just fabrications, or perhaps artifacts of consciousness? Or, did they point to another dimension that only consciousness could enter? There were many stories of making contact with such entities, but this left me only wanting to go deeper, beneath the surface.

Naturally, my examination turned toward awareness itself. This is where things got sticky, so to speak. Reality was a moving target that many had tried to explain, but none convincingly. How, for example, could anyone explain Katerina's experience of an all-knowing guru who saw her mother's death? Could any theory of consciousness account for hundreds of near death experiences, or NDEs?

Jung, for example, posited that individual unconscious arose out of the structure of an unconscious that cannot be grasped or truly seen. This would be akin to seeing the shadow of something, but never seeing the actual object from which the shadow was made. Jung even envisioned aliens and UFOs as a "modern myth" that came about because we seemed incapable of dealing with our earthly demons. So, why not project our unsolvable problems onto an external power or phenomenon that was beyond our ability to grasp, such as aliens?

The scientific reductionists, on the other hand, believed that we were simply biological machines, digesting the molecules required for life and nothing more. From this perspective, the firing of synapses and EEG brain waves conjured up artifacts such as perceptions and thoughts, which were responsible for creating a false sense of personhood and consciousness.

By the end of the week, my head was swimming in contradictory beliefs and theories. Consciousness was a topic that many philosophers and scientists had spent years studying, so I didn't hope to find a definitive answer. It seemed fair to say, however, that the problem with *any* of these approaches was that they attempted to decode what was, at its essence, supremely subjective and personal. Because of my own experiences over the past few days, I was at peace with knowing there were ways of seeing and understanding that science could not fathom, and maybe never would. That was good enough for me.

It was nearly 5:00 pm when I packed up my belongings and put them in the car. Moments later I sat on a wooden bench on the library grounds, rubbing my bleary eyes. I was preparing myself to tell Beth the truth about why I got fired when I got home later that evening. What would I say? How would she respond? I couldn't believe the devastating turn that my whole life had taken.

I looked up to see the western sky blotted with dabs of purple, red and yellow, as if someone had taken out a gigantic highlighter and swiped it on the clouds. Sitting there, I tried to be with each breath. Just to notice how it entered the body. How the body moved. Then how it left the body. It was enough to give me a moment's space and solace from my stuckness. I recalled how many of the techniques I'd utilized in my clinical work were based on the mind. But whose mind? Was I simply trying to convince others to drink my own cognitive-based Kool-Aid? I breathed out, trying to let go of this line of thinking, as well as all mental concepts. Each time a thought entered my head, I just mentally repeated the word "releasing" as I exhaled it out.

After maybe a half hour or more of this, thoughts became fewer. My gaze softened and the surroundings grew hazier and hazier, until the entire landscape, Fire Station 15, the sky, all of it seemed covered in white gauze, as if it had all been bleached or washed out. I felt as if something deep inside of me had attained a still point, a perfectly balanced and unshakeable equilibrium.

At that moment, a tingling at the base of my spine seemed to burst, and I felt a powerful eruption of energy rush up my spine. Next, my head shuddered involuntarily as the energy surged first in my occipital lobe at the back of my head. The vibration grew into a deep and resonant rumble, like a freight train moving through my head. The sound swelled along the temporal lobes at the sides, then finally enveloped the frontal cortex. Just when I wasn't sure if I could tolerate the intensity, the vibration transformed into an oscillating wave that swelled and ebbed in my head, along with a strange gurgling and bubbling sound. The oscillating wave started moving throughout my entire body, from my head to my toes, and then back up. The only thought I had was that this must be my etheric essence or life energy, the source from which my being was animated. It was vital, alive.

That's when it came into focus.

Before me glowed an otherworldly dimension of multi-layered pearly strands, almost like mist or rainfall. It was similar, but different from the mind meld experience I had with Traveler Jacki. What was this place? Here, it seemed as if everything was infused with light energy. I knew that what was before me was too real to be imaginary. Just then, the words of Vivekananda echoed through my being: *The infinite library of the universe is in your own mind.*

That's when I wondered: Could my energy body gain access to this multi-layered dimension?

With that single thought, I was instantly transported inside the living, vibrating dimension that seemed to extend indefinitely. The dimension quivered with each breath and movement I made. When I raised my hand to touch one of the thin, milky and dewy strands, a ripple immediately pulsated throughout the entire dimensional space. I experimented, and found that even the smallest movement, even tensing my facial muscles, created a barely discernible pulse that seemed to travel through the entire dimension.

Then, a particular memory came to me, and I'm not sure why. But as I recalled the struggles I endured during my medical residency, a dim flickering image of myself from that time period suddenly materialized in the distance. This younger me, looking depressed, stressed and undernourished, wore blue hospital scrubs in the ER. When I placed my attention on him, I traveled instantaneously to the image, and we were suddenly face to face, as if in the present moment. Though I don't think he (the younger me) could see me, I mentally sent him the strong intention of self-care, that he needed to start caring for his own well-being. It felt like a beam of this positive energy was coming out of me and pouring into the younger, distressed me.

Oddly, it occurred to me how, as a resident, out of the blue I'd started exercising, eating and sleeping better. Why had I done that? Did that impulse actually come from a future self — *the me who was right here, right now?*

I wasn't with my past self for long, however, because the moment I wondered if this could work in reverse, my attention was immediately drawn to the shimmering image of an old man, someone oddly familiar.

Again, placing my attention on him brought us face to face. The white hair, the pallid complexion and the wrinkled skin were those of an old man. But the eyes twinkled with the playfulness and insatiable wonderment of a child. Suddenly, I knew this was me, some twenty-five or thirty years into the future. Although we didn't speak, I could feel myself being touched by his sense of curiosity, love, contentment and lightness. Was that my future self's message to me?

Next, the word *Jesus* popped into my head.

Don't ask me why. All I knew was that a sudden and immense, earthquake-like tremor surged throughout the entire dimension, lighting it up and suffusing it with energy. That a single word could contain so much power frightened me, and that's when I was jolted back to my normal consciousness as a guy sitting on a bench by the library.

A man walked past and said hello, but I was still in such a state of shock that I couldn't utter a word. I took a few deep breaths to recollect myself, even squeezing the wooden slats on the bench with my hands to make sure my reality was solid. Thankfully, it was.

I desperately wanted to make sense of my experience. But how could anyone hope to describe something as ineffable as a *library of the universe*? Sitting on that bench, I suddenly felt immersed in a mystery far greater than myself. It seemed like the universe was a quantum collective, a place where — somehow — consciousness itself acted as the primordial organizing energy capable of storing information and materializing as matter, and where everything, including the past and future, existed and intermingled as one, inseparable.

I tried to imagine what others would have thought if they had experienced this. Would they have conjectured that it was *how* you tapped into that collective that determined which reality would be expressed and manifested? I didn't know if I'd ever access this dimension again, but as far as I could tell, the slightest energy, thought or movement was transmitted instantly throughout the quantum collective, touching and affecting everything else.

One thing was for certain: The infinite library of the universe was no longer a concept in my mind, but as real to me as any physical object. Still, I questioned how long this "revelation" would stay with me or how it might change me, my perceptions of things, and my relationships. For the rest of the evening, I moved around the house super slowly and cautiously, questioning whether my actions in this reality affected the more subtle dimension. Beth could tell something was up when

I skipped dinner and my evening glass of red wine. When she asked me if everything was okay at the hospital, I fumbled for words, vaguely mentioning some "issues" at the hospital. Although I had planned on telling her about getting fired, my experience on the bench had dramatically transformed my mental landscape. All of a sudden, my job situation seemed a lot less important than it did a couple of days before.

I sat outside under the backyard awning, reflecting on my experience. I was shocked that the past and present were not fixed as I'd been taught, but that they could fluidly interact. The led me to consider if there was a way to reconcile, perhaps even integrate spirit, healing and psychotherapy. I could only guess at how many people had tapped the infinite library, only to tell a doctor and wrongly end up on seizure medication or in a mental hospital.

The idea of integrating the *Traveler's eye* with medicine made sense to me. Wouldn't a deeper understanding of our experiences and imaginal realms stimulate a more cohesive awareness of our story as evolving beings in a conscious universe?

My train of thought was broken as the rain rapped ever more loudly on the awning. I had a sudden and strong impulse that I needed to find Traveler Jacki. Previously, I might have ignored such inner signals, but something told me not to wait. I put on my rain jacket and hat, and told Beth I'd be back, and not to worry. She did worry, though. She followed me into the garage and handed me my hiking boots.

"What are these for?"

"You never know when you might need them," she said, presaging my visit to Jacki, even though I hadn't mentioned it.

I didn't say anything, but just looked at her. Each moment seemed like a priceless treasure to me now, and I didn't want to let go of this one, even though I had to. I leaned forward and just held her tightly. I climbed into the car and started the engine. Before I backed out of the driveway, I leaned my head out the window.

"Beth, I lost my job, I got fired! It's a good thing!"

"You got what??"

Her face froze in an expression of alarm as I quickly backed out onto the street. As I drove away, she ran after the car, calling out.

"Promise me you won't do anything crazy!"

Chapter 25

The hospital grounds were aglow with nighttime construction lights, which illuminated sheets of falling rain. The no trespassing tape and stanchions had been replaced with an eight-foot high chain linked fence. The cottage was dark inside, but I knocked lightly on the door anyway. A light went on, and Jacki opened the door, inviting me inside.

Traveler Jacki had heard about my leaving the hospital and asked what happened. I told her my version of events, without giving away specific names because of confidentiality. I made it clear, however, that I believed a *certain* candidate for Oregon Attorney General had made a deal with a *certain* Executive Director to keep a *certain* young man, who may or may not be a patient at a *certain* hospital, quiet. *Wink, wink.*

I looked around and saw there was no food in the cottage. When I offered to get some snacks from the local market, Traveler Jacki refused, saying their meal vouchers would be good enough until they had to leave. That's when I learned that she'd been given a notice of two weeks. She'd agreed to maintain the garden until that time.

"But what about the treasure?" I asked.

"I started digging, but then they put up that fence."

"Do you still have access to the gardening shed?"

"Yeah, I think so."

"Wait a sec." I crouched down and put on my hiking boots. Moments later, in the gardening shed, I fetched a wire cutter and an eight-foot ladder. We each grabbed a shovel for good measure. We shut the door to the shed and cautiously made our way back to the construction site.

"You see anyone patrolling?" I leaned the ladder against the fence and snipped away a nasty-looking strand of razor wire that was strung across the top.

"Nah, just a hospital guard who comes out from time to time."

"Good." I knew we'd be okay so long as my buddy Jeff was on duty.

We were partially shadowed by large equipment as we dug in the area that Mason had identified. The rain was persistent, and my hands kept slipping off the slick shovel handle. I kept at it until my shovel made a loud clinking sound.

"I hit something." I put my boot on the shovel to push it further into the soft ground.

"No, don't," warned Jacki, "we need to go slow."

"Why?"

"It's what the Old Ones are telling me." Traveler Jacki bent down and carefully scraped away the soil. I set down my shovel and helped. Even Bear jumped into the pit, using his paws to dig out the mud.

Jacki pulled up what looked like a cane handle with marks on it. Then, she found some other misshaped objects.

"This is it! This is what we was lookin' for." She handed the two fragments to me, which I examined closely.

"Really? I don't think this is a treasure."

"This is why the Old Ones called."

Just then, the sound of a voice on a bullhorn jolted us. "This is security. You are trespassing. Do not attempt to run!"

"Run, Jacki! I'll distract him." I stood up waving my hands. "I'm over here. Don't shoot." I waved my arms, the muddy objects still in my hands. In the glare of the flashlight, I saw who it was. Unfortunately, it wasn't Jeff, but the other guard, Danny.

"Danny, is that you? It's me, Dr. Banks."

"What the hell are you doing here, Banks? This is off limits."

"I, uhm, dropped some keys around here the other day. So, I thought..."

"What's that? In your hands?"

"It's nothing. Nothing."

"That is hospital property. Drop it now," he demanded.

"Hey, Danny, come on. Can you help me out here?"

"Help you? You broke into Dr. Howell's office. You were fired, thrown off the premises and now you want me to help you? I'll call the police if I have to."

"Danny, I think I found something important here. I don't know what it is, but you have to inform Dr. Howell. They have to stop construction immediately."

"Don't make me do something we'll both end up regretting." Danny drew his gun. "For the last time. Drop what you have there."

Out of the corner of my eye, I saw Bear. I didn't know what to do, so I threw the two artifacts at Bear, as if a spaniel would know what to do. But Bear ran and grabbed each item in his mouth.

"Run, Bear, run!" I shouted.

"That's hospital property. Stop!" screamed Danny.

Bear followed a serpentine route around construction machinery as Danny hopelessly tried to keep up. I ran to the unlocked front gate from where Danny had entered, got into my car and sped off. In my rearview mirror, I thought I saw Danny waving at Bear, who was sprinting full-speed down the street.

After driving aimlessly for a few blocks I pulled over. My

body's sympathetic nervous system was running full tilt. Every cell tingled with hypervigilance. I felt suddenly faint as my head was crammed with questions. Would the police be coming by my house to arrest me? Should I turn myself in? What were those muddy objects? How could we halt construction?

I was worried about returning home because I didn't want to incriminate Beth or place her in harm's way. Escapist behavior wasn't exactly the kind of advice I'd give patients who were facing difficulties, but it seemed prudent, at least for the evening. Besides, I doubted Danny would call the police or make any official report.

As I pondered where to stay for the night, I noticed the flashing sign of the Rose City Shelter about a half block up the street. Normally, I'd have eschewed staying at such a place. But now, I wondered if the people staying here weren't really Travelers, at least in the sense that they saw things a little bit differently. From that perspective, it felt like coming home.

Chapter 26

I recognized the same woman tending the front desk as before, but today she was sporting a blue and yellow bandana over her hair. I wondered whether Jacki had left the cottage but I couldn't be sure. Could she have come here?

"I'm looking for a woman with a feather and a dog."

"To each his own," she said, giving me the once over. "This here's all we got." She motioned towards the few people mulling around.

"No, that's not what I... Can I just get a room?"

"*That* we got." She chewed gum and snapped big pink bubbles the entire time she took my information.

The elevator was out of order, so I trudged up five floors along a creaky and dim staircase. The room had only one light bulb, making it hard to determine the color of the walls. I pushed aside the curtain covering the solitary window and found myself staring at a brown brick wall of the adjacent building. The bed was a single, with a threadbare blanket. There was no water or bath other than the shared bathroom at the end of the hall. It didn't make much difference since I had no toiletries or belongings to speak of.

I sent Beth a text, letting her know that I had to "lay low" for a day, and that she shouldn't worry if the police came looking for me.

She texted me back: "WTF! Laying low??"

I realized that my choice of words made things sound as if I were on the run after a criminal act. But in fact, I had broken into a locked construction site with a sign that said *No Trespassing— Violators Will Be Prosecuted*. After trying to calm her down, as well as calm myself, I lay down on the bed, which was actually more comfortable than my sofa sleeper. Soon, my body started to relax. I had just closed my eyes when my phone rang. It was Shirley Delabrey.

Shirley's voice cracked as she spoke, and I couldn't tell whether she was frantic or frightened. But she had taken my advice and visited Mason. She was dismayed by his condition and didn't know what to do. Given that I was no longer working at the hospital, I suggested we meet at a small Irish pub that I knew was open late in Lake Oswego, an upscale community where the Delabrey family lived.

"And, Shirley? Bring Mason's phone with you."

The pub was dark, crowded and noisy. A group of men and women tossed darts at a board, while a band of three musicians played spirited, foot-stomping Irish folk songs on a small stage. I found some empty seats in the corner, as far from the band as possible. I was only there a couple of minutes when Shirley came in. But she wasn't alone. Mason's older brother, Eddie, was with her.

They sat, and we ordered soft drinks all around. Shirley removed a green silk scarf from her head and settled in. She looked around nervously, as if expecting her husband to show up any minute. Finally, she spoke up.

"When I saw Mason, it frightened me. You were right. He's so not him. Edward was appointed as Mason's guardian so he makes all the decisions. But that's why I brought Eddie."

"I don't understand."

"Eddie? Tell Dr. Banks what you know."

Eddie squirmed uncomfortably in his chair. He explained that it was his father who had taken the pellet gun from Mason's room that day and had egged Eddie on to "play a joke" on Mason. According to Eddie, both he and his dad knew the gun was harmless and without any pellets. Eddie admitted that he incited the situation by pointing the gun at Mason and Jodi. It turned out that Mason responded to the threat in order to protect his friend.

After hearing the story, I asked if Eddie was willing to withdraw his complaint against his brother and tell the police the truth. He answered in the affirmative, and I asked him to do that first thing in the morning.

"One last thing. Did you bring Mason's phone?"

"Yes." Shirley told me the code as she handed it over.

"You did the right thing, Eddie. For you and your brother. I'll be in touch." I took my wallet and slapped down some cash for the bill and tip.

Back in my car, I scanned through the contact list on Mason's phone until I found Jodi. Call it a hunch, but I felt I needed to get her side of the story. I left a voicemail, and a few minutes later, when I was preparing to text her, she called back.

"Jodi, this is Dr. Banks. I was Mason's doctor before he was arrested."

"What do you want?"

"I'm worried about Mason, and I need your help."

"Come to my house. My parents are home, so I'll meet you outside."

I waited at the curb of a split-level suburban home. A small-framed girl came down the steps holding an umbrella. Jodi had an oval-shaped face, framed by light blonde hair and a long streak of blue that accentuated her large crystal blue, almond-shaped eyes. She shook my hand, then asked about Mason. But instead of answering, I found it disconcerting that two people kept staring at us from the window.

"Are those..."

"My parents, yeah."

"Maybe I should go and explain..."

"Nah. They already know you're my drug dealer."

"Jodi, I'm not even supposed to be talking with you, because of confidentiality."

"Yeah, I know all about that shit. I won't tell anyone."

"Okay. Well, I was hoping you could tell me what happened that night."

"No, I can't."

"No?"

"Yeah, because I'd rather show you. When Mason's brother knocked on the door, I thought he was a total tool, so I started recording him."

Jodi had caught the entire episode. The clip clearly showed Eddie Jr. taunting his brother and pointing the gun at him. It showed the struggle, and also Edward Delabrey joining the fracas and kicking his son in the stomach and chest several times. As Mason and Jodi ran down the staircase, the camera angled up on Edward Delabrey as he sneered down at Mason and said, "No one fucks with my campaign. No one."

My heart skipped. "Did you show this to anyone?"

"No way. I didn't want to make things worse for Mason. His asshole father gets away with shit like you wouldn't believe."

"Not this time. I promise. Are you willing to post this?"

"I don't know," muttered Jodi, giving me a wary look.

"You have to trust me. It could be Mason's only chance."

Jodi nodded almost imperceptibly, then slyly grinned as her fingers darted over her phone. As I held her umbrella to keep us dry, Jodi sent the video out to her own favorite social media outlets.

❋

I got up late, after nine, unshaven, mud-caked and crumpled. I washed my mouth out with water. Down at the front desk I asked if they had any toothpaste. The morning clerk was a thin, balding man who leaned down to look under the counter. He surfaced and handed me the smallest tube of toothpaste I had ever seen.

I spent a moment perusing the lobby. A few people slowly moved about. One woman was curled up on a chair, trying to stay warm. A middle-aged man wearing torn jeans and a flannel black and white shirt walked up and asked if I could buy him some food from the vending machine. I bought some cheese crackers. When he said the words "Bless you," he smiled crookedly, his wrinkled face showing years of struggle.

That was when I decided to come back here and volunteer however I could for the less fortunate Travelers of this world. As I walked back past the front desk, I heard the desk clerk chuckle.

"Hey, you seen this?" he said, nodding at the TV on the wall. "And this guy's running for Attorney General?"

I spun around to see Jodi's video clip. I was transfixed when the clip ended and the news anchor announced that a reporter was waiting outside Edward Delabrey's law office. Indeed, a gauntlet of local media pundits, reporters and camera operators blocked the entrance. There was a whirlwind of excitement as Delabrey approached carrying his briefcase, trying not to look flustered. A barrage of questions ricocheted at him from all sides.

"Did you set up your son with up a phony assault charge?"

"Why were you kicking him?"

"Where is your son right now? Did you get him committed?"

"Did you know that the gun had no pellets?"

"Why are you stigmatizing the mental health community?"

"Can we talk to your son?"

"Did you trump up the charge on your son?"

Unable to control himself, Delabrey scowled angrily, "No I will not talk about my son! I have done nothing wrong! He was charged with a violent crime, and if you care to check, you'll find I have donated very generously to the mental hospital where he's staying."

Like a halfback diving for the end zone, Delabrey literally shouldered two reporters out of the way and entered his office, slamming the door behind him. The reporter finished his report:

"There you have it. The candidate for Attorney General refusing to answer questions or give any details about the condition of his son and a possible cover-up. This is Ross Hilton. Back to you in the studio."

"That was the scene earlier this morning at Edward Delabrey's downtown law office. We'll keep you updated on any further news."

In the bathroom, I swished the minty toothpaste in my mouth, wondering what my next step would be. I thought there was a good chance we could push for a review of Mason's mental commitment hold, even a reversal. Truth was, I was still pondering whether to show my face at the hospital when my friend from forensics called.

"Hey, Bob, I guess you saw the news?"

"I'm calling because they just took Mason down to the sterile procedure room, and I thought you should know."

"Procedure room? Why?"

"It's for an ECT."

"What?... Electroconvulsive therapy? Are you sure?"

"Absolutely."

"Oh, no, that can't be. That's fucked up!"

"I agree."

"What about family consent?"

"I just spoke with the mom. But she's not the guardian. It's the father."

"Shit. But you're the attending. You can override it, Bob."

"I can't, Ben. Beverly ordered it. I tried to dissuade her, but she said it was already on the docket and necessary. It sucks. Anyway, I thought you should know." His voice was tinged with a tone of resignation.

"Bob, can you get me into the procedure room? You gotta get me in," I yelled in frustration as I bounded down the five floors of narrow, dimly lit stairs two and three steps at a time.

"Are you crazy? Today's the Board of Directors' meeting. You know what a mess it is with all the C-suite people up here in the auditorium. As far as getting in and out, this place might as well be on lockdown."

"What time's the procedure scheduled for?"

"Ten."

When I reached ground level, I looked up at the large analog clock behind the front desk. It was already 9:45 am. I was breathless as I spoke. "Damn. So, who's going to be in the room?" "Beverly's conducting the ECT, then there's Fredo, and Brenda's the anesthesiologist."

"One last favor, Bob?"

"You're killing me, Ben. I mean, you literally are gonna kill me one of these days."

"You gotta find Jeff, the security officer and have him call me immediately. Got it? Have him call this number."

I jumped in my car. My best chance for entry, I figured, was from the loading dock. As I wheeled over to the hospital, I couldn't stop thinking about the irreparable damage ECT would do to Mason. While ECT had been found to be beneficial for treatment resistant depression, it was inappropriate to use on a teenager who hadn't already exhausted all other available options. From my perspective, giving ECT to a developing brain was basically like performing an electrical lobotomy. I had read several studies that detected brain damage and reduced brain connectivity afterwards. ECT sent surges of electricity into the brain's prefrontal cortex—the most evolved and human part of the brain that made empathy, love and insight possible. I could only pray I wasn't too late.

I screeched up next to a food service truck. The dock was humming with activity because of the Board of Directors' meeting, which included a catered brunch from outside the hospital. I walked over to one truck and found a paper hat worn by food staff. Then, I grabbed a stainless-steel food tray and raised it up to cover my face. If I had learned one thing from my investigation of Sasquatch's elopement, it was that food handlers enjoyed almost unlimited movement around the hospital.

Chapter 27

Once inside, I went to the uniform closet and donned a food preparer's jacket. Properly attired, I went back to forensics with my food tray. I punched in the code, relieved to find that it still worked. Inside the unit I moved about unobtrusively, until I spied Sasquatch near the empty nurses' station. All it took was one look at the food, and the big man willingly followed me out of the unit. We walked to the nearest exit. Then, after giving Sasquatch a club sandwich, I let him outside, to meander in an open field.

It was now about five minutes to ten. I snaked through the halls, even passing a couple of people who I worried would identify me. Fortunately, my food handler's disguise was effective. My senses were hyperalert as I gingerly stepped inside a utility closet that was right next door to the procedure room. My breathing was rapid and uneven as I picked up the hospital phone. I tried to calm down but couldn't.

There was no backing out now, I realized, as I punched in a few buttons to activate the intercom. "Elopement on the exterior grounds by the forensics unit. Patient elopement! Check for missing forensic patient. Respond immediately," I declared in a low voice.

When I heard a door open, I peeked out of the closet to watch as Fredo hurriedly left the premises to answer the elopement call. A strange feeling overcame me as I gripped the door handle of the procedure room. Even though I was about to face my own dragon, so to speak, I felt a pervading sense of calm and confidence. I had always avoided upsetting the order of things. Now, I was ready to fight the good fight, and to hell with the aftermath.

I swung open the door, and saw that Beverly was preparing for a bi-temporal ECT, which meant she would attach an electrode to each of Mason's temples. The right electrode was already affixed.

"Stop this procedure immediately, Beverly."

"Are you a doctor? Do you even work here?" she snarled contemptuously. "Oh wait a minute. You've been banned by your licensing board and fired. So, you wouldn't have the faintest idea of what's best for him, would you?"

"Or maybe what's best for you? Was this your deal with Delabrey? To shut Mason up?"

"You are truly delusional. You know that? Brenda, is the patient unconscious yet?"

"Not quite, ma'am," replied the anesthesiologist. Just then, Mason stirred on the gurney.

"Well, it'll have to be good enough. Now, Brenda, call for help! Get security in here."

I scanned the room and saw an open case with syringes. I picked up a familiar IM, the one with Haldol. "Have you ever been IM'd Beverly? I hear it's very relaxing."

Brenda carefully scooted around me as Beverly placed the second electrode on Mason's left temple. I must have been at least fifteen feet away, too late to stop her from flicking the switch on the ECT unit. But, just as I was about to rush Beverly, I thought I saw a grayish mass materialize over her head. I blinked, thinking this was a really crappy time to start hallucinating.

Crystallizing into form and zig-zagging toward me was an ominous, shark-like creature with rows of razor blade teeth and eyes blacker than death. My mind instantly flashed on Sasquatch's assault of Beverly when he was shouting "kill the shark" and jabbing his knife at a seemingly invisible adversary. *Was this what he saw?*

As if from nowhere, my own battalion of butterflies materialized and assumed a sledgehammer shape. The two forms attacked and jabbed at each other. The shark's thick fin pinned the butterflies against the ceiling. Just when the jagged teeth appeared ready to bite, the butterflies shape-shifted into a tornado that funneled into the creature's mouth, then balling up and gagging it. The shark thrashed helplessly, futilely fighting for breath. Finally, with a giant shudder, its eyes rolled up in its head, and it sunk down, lifeless.

Thunderstruck, as if no time had passed, I suddenly found myself standing face to face with Beverly. I couldn't grasp how I had gotten so close. Her eyes burned fiery red, and I swear she hissed at me as I grabbed her hand that was but a hair's width from frying Mason's brain. It wasn't without some pleasure that I plunged the IM into her arm. Within seconds, she drooped onto a chair like a melted frozen yogurt.

I shook my head, wondering what had just happened when a single, luminous butterfly wafted down and landed on my hand. I broke into a smile and guffawed. Then, as mysteriously as it had come into being, the delicate creature left with a flutter, its wings leaving behind only tracings of light resembling a sparkler. I stood there, incredulous, just as Brenda arrived with the guard. I was relieved to see it was Jeff.

Quickly, I removed the electrodes from Mason's temples. "So tell me, Jeff, did you get it?"

"Oh yeah. Got it, Doc, right here." He raised his closed fist in the air. Brenda looked surprised when Jeff didn't pull his gun. But she was aghast at seeing Dr. Howell nearly unconscious.

"Brenda, can you please help us wake Mason up?"

"Oh my God… What happened to…?"

"Oh, Dr. Howell? She, uhm… she went to her safe place."

Within a few minutes, Mason was groggy, but able to walk. I called Dr. Bob and told him where to find Mason, and to wait with him in my office. Meanwhile, Jeff and I maneuvered a gurney that carried a prostrate Dr. Howell.

We opened the double doors to the auditorium as the Board of Directors' meeting was getting underway. A large table on the stage of the auditorium was overflowing with croissants, pastries, juices, quiche, assorted berries and fruit, roast beef and even champagne, no doubt to toast the new hospital addition.

"Where's Beverly? Did anyone get a text?" The woman sitting at the head of the table checked her phone.

"Don't bother. She's right here!" I moved the gurney into position where the board members could view it.

What followed was a horror-struck response of shrieks and yelps.

"Don't worry, she's fine, just a little marinated in Haldol," I motioned to Jeff. "What do you say we put that video on the screen."

"You!?" A board member recoiled while pointing at me. "You're the one who got fired for stealing. Beverly told us about that. Call the police!"

"People, hold on," interrupted Jeff, assuming control and being more authoritative than I'd ever seen him. "Dr. Banks didn't do anything wrong." Jeff plugged the flash drive into the auditorium computer and played the video clip on a large screen. "I got this off Dr. Howell's office security cam."

In the clip, Delabrey and Dr. Howell spoke clandestinely about what each of them needed. As I had suspected, Delabrey promised to fund the expansion so long as Dr. Howell "kept the boy quiet" during his election campaign. Near the end clip, Beverly put one hand to each of her temples and said, "Don't worry, Edward. I'll give him an electric shock guaranteed to leave him speechless."

From the gurney, Beverly pointed and vainly tried to make a point, but only spittle and drool dribbled down her chin. There was a lot of heated back and forth discussion by the board about what to do. They heard from me about how she had conspired with Edward Delabrey, almost severely harmed Mason, and tried to hide a Code Silver event from the Joint Commission. Only one board member wanted to place Beverly on administrative leave. All the others were disgusted by her actions and wanted her removed immediately. I was surprised when they took a vote and fired her on the spot.

Jeff and I left the meeting and took Dr. Howell to the front entrance. She was still highly sedated, but able to stumble by the time we placed her in a hospital van to take her home. As the van pulled away, I noticed a construction foreman angrily waving his hands while talking with Traveler Jacki and a tall man I'd never seen before. Then, the foreman came storming up to the front desk, demanding to see Beverly. When he was told she was no longer in charge, he huffed, "We have no choice but to pull our crew." Within minutes, several trucks left the site, churning up a choking cloud of gravel, smoke and dust.

While watching the evacuation, someone grabbed my arm. It was Traveler Jacki, standing alongside the tall man in a suit.

"Traveler Ben, this is Gerald."

"Gerald Long, from the BIA."

"BIA?" I inquired.

"Bureau of Indian Affairs," he said, handing me his card.

"What's this all about?"

"Those artifacts you found are from a sacred native burial ground. I thank you, and the ancestors thank you, for protecting this special ground."

I was stunned, and suddenly it dawned on me that we had to inform the Board of Directors. "Gerald, there are some people we need to tell about this." We all returned to the auditorium. When Gerald presented his findings, the C-suiters appeared shell-shocked. After the board unanimously voted to cease the hospital expansion, I thought they all could have benefitted from a process group to explore their emotions.

I bid farewell to Gerald near the burial site. Without the construction trucks, the grounds felt serene and at peace. I looked at Jacki in amazement.

"How about that. So there really was a treasure."

Traveler Jacki's eyes sparkled as she nodded. The long, white feather in her tassel shone brightly in the sun as she reached out and took both my hands.

"It was real special getting to know you, Traveler Ben. I speak for Bear, too." Bear yowled loudly, speaking for himself.

"Wait, what do you mean?"

"Me and Bear, our work here is done."

"Done… you mean finding the treasure?"

Traveler Jacki's eyebrows raised slightly. "Not exactly. That's not really why we was here. You see… we came here because of you, Traveler Ben. It was *your* spirit we heard calling for help."

"*My* spirit? Huh… I don't understand," I said, confounded. "But you heard the ancient Old Ones calling. You said so."

"Yeah, of course we heard 'em. But it was *you* who called the loudest, ain't that right, Bear?" She leaned forward, gave me a long hug and kissed me on the cheek. Bear, from his shoulder perch, nuzzled my neck. Traveler Jackie's eyes were moist as she let me go. Slowly, she turned to leave.

"Wait. Wait, you can't go. You haven't said why…" I started to follow her when I got an urgent text from Dr. Bob. I'd totally forgotten that I left him waiting in my office with Mason! "We have to talk. You wait here for me, okay?! Promise not to go anywhere," I called over my shoulder at Traveler Jacki as I ran back inside.

After debriefing events with Bob, we agreed that it would be in Mason's best interests to be released, pending the reversal of the assault charges. A few well-placed calls to the Clackamas County Sheriff's Office assured us that charges were already being dropped. Even better, we learned that Mason's guardianship had just been transferred to Shirley. In fact, the coming days would have a disgraced Edward Delabrey quitting the race for Attorney General.

On the spot, we conjured up a discharge plan that had Mason seeing a private clinician, as well as being enrolled in DBT groups or Art Therapy groups as needed.

"Hellooo, I'm in the room," waved Mason. "I can hear you guys. Where will I go? Because I'm definitely not going back home. I've been wasting my time there. I gotta get out and see what life is really about."

"I agree, Mason. We'll figure it out," I said with a surprised expression on my face, glad to see that Mason had proactively stood up for himself. His eyes appeared less occluded, brighter. His facial expressions were more animated; he was more energized and purposeful in a way that made him seem like an entirely different person. I could hardly believe the change since Traveler Jacki worked on him. Well, that and going off the anti-psychotic meds. I knew there would be a lot to consider in the coming days.

Bob escorted Mason back to his room as I finally prepared to leave the premises. But Fran corralled me in the hallway. "Dr. Banks, I've been looking all over for you. They want you back in the auditorium. Like, right now."

I couldn't imagine why I was being asked back *again*, especially after I'd shot their next President to-be full of Haldol and foiled their plans for expansion. The hospital board asked me to sit down with them. They then shared, in rather emotional terms, the realization of how dangerously close the organization had been to losing its purpose and mission. What came next shocked me. They wanted to steady the ship, and they asked if I would assume the now vacated position of Executive Director, and possibly consider more responsibility in the future. I sat silent for a long period of time.

"I don't know what to say. I'm really, really honored that you asked me. But there's someone who I think would make the perfect Executive Director. His name is Dr. Robert Trent. He's dedicated, honest and he cares about the patients. But if you decide on him, I want to be the first to tell him because he's done a few favors for me."

After departing from my first and maybe last Board of Directors' meeting, I rushed back outside to find Traveler Jacki. I looked everywhere, from the stone cottage to the tool shed. Frantically, I went into the chapel, thinking she might have gone there. Chaplain Joyce hadn't seen her either, so I asked our receptionist, Fran, and others by the entrance, but Traveler Jacki was gone. And she and Bear had left no tracks. I was disheartened at not being able to talk with her. The last words she spoke kept echoing in my head.

We came here because of you, Traveler Ben. It was your spirit we heard calling for help.

But why? And why me? I recalled Katerina's description of guiding intelligent energies that existed in the universe. Had I just been contacted by one? Or two, if you counted Bear. Had Traveler Jacki acted as a catalyst who moved me out of darkness when nothing else could? A slight, tingling shudder moved from the base of my skull and down my spine, and for a moment my mind stopped. Strange as it sounds, I had the sense of Traveler Jacki and Bear being nearby. But when I looked around, they were nowhere in sight.

Yes, I should also mention that I *did* tell Bob the good news, and he was thrilled to take on the challenge of being the Executive Director. It felt good to do something for him, especially after all the times he stepped out on a limb for me.

There was, however, still one other important debt I needed to repay.

Chapter 28

Beth was appalled. My boots and pants were still caked in mud from digging for the treasure. My clothes also looked, quite correctly, as if I'd slept in them. She made me some tea and pressed for details about my being fired and my worrisome messages about "laying low." She was even more shocked to hear how I'd saved Mason from ECT and that I'd dosed our Executive Director with a powerful tranquilizer.

"I never liked that woman," confided Beth, sitting close to me and shaking her head. "Oh my God. Look at you. Breaking and entering. Saving people. Tranquilizing your boss. You are definitely not the same man I've been married to for twenty-four years."

"Is that a bad thing?"

"I don't know."

"Beth, I'm not sure if I want to go back to work."

"Because of the license?"

"Nah, that'll get cleared up. But I've been thinking. We should travel, see things. Kivas in New Mexico, geysers in Yellowstone, glaciers in Alaska."

"Are you serious? You never wanted to leave the house.

Besides, what about my job?"

"You could take a sabbatical. There has to be a better way to live."

Beth grew silent, and her head dropped. I lifted her chin and saw she was sniffling.

"What?"

"Today... it's Mel's anniversary."

I reached out and took Beth's hands in mine. We sat in silence for what felt like an hour. Finally, she let go a long sigh.

"Oh, I'm sorry. I'm so sorry, Beth. And here I am talking about traveling."

"Well, Ben, that's what Melissa would be doing if she was here. She wanted to see all those places you mentioned."

In the afternoon, we went to the cemetery together. We placed a large bouquet of flowers at the gravesite. Beth and I looked at each other as we held hands.

"Our baby's here, with us," she said, blinking away tears.

"I know. I can feel her, too. She's with me, wherever I go."

Later, while sitting in Mel's room with Beth, I surprised her with the delicate rose quartz pendant necklace given to me by Traveler Jacki. Beth pointed out how it was pink, just like Mel's favorite color. I didn't say anything, but I could only speculate whether Traveler Jacki had known that.

Over a glass of wine, we decided to take our trip, though exactly when and for how long we weren't sure. It was strange, but I felt the same way I did as when I first met Beth. There was an excitement, a joy, a delight in her presence. We snuggled that evening on the sofa in front of a blazing fireplace.

That night I had a vivid dream. I thought I saw Mason doing a remote, out-of-body flyover, checking me out to see how I was. When I awoke, I had the distinct feeling that he was free, whatever that meant.

Chapter 29

I made my signature spinach omelet for Beth the next morning. Five whipped eggs, sautéed spinach in olive oil with a clove of garlic, salt and pepper to taste. During breakfast, I posed the possibility of us taking in a border, maybe a college-aged student who was in need of a loving and caring place to stay.

"Where, in Melissa's room?"

"Maybe. I'm just floating the idea."

Beth, of course, knew exactly where I was headed with this, and said she needed to meet Mason first.

"But wouldn't that be a dual relationship with a patient?"

"True. But that only counts if I'm a doctor."

"Are you *really* Benjamin Banks?" She smiled and kissed me hard on the mouth.

That morning, believe it or not, I headed straight to the hospital for my job. Yes, after assuming his new job as Executive Director, Bob's first act was to reinstate me. I admit that I was ambivalent about coming back to a caregiving role that seemed inherently flawed. But Bob, who was an expert at motivational interviewing, also known as *change talk*, turned my disillusionment around. He affirmed my doubts and concerns

221

about the checklist method of care, and let me feel heard. Bob was surprised, however, when I told him I wanted to return to forensics.

"Really?" Bob's head tilted askance for a moment. "Hmmm... I didn't think you liked working with psychotic patients. Not to mention violent."

"I uhm... had a recent change of heart, Bob," I answered with a smile and a wink. After Bob promised to transition me to forensics, I shared that my return to the hospital needed to be conditional, at least until I had more time to reflect on where and what I wanted to do. Thankfully, he was fully onboard. And, I still planned on helping out at the Rose City Shelter whenever possible.

My first day back at the clinic was uneventful, except for asking if anyone had seen Traveler Jacki and Bear. No one had. Neither could I locate Mason during my morning rounds, but apparently he wasn't yet assigned a room in the adult clinic. I planned to check into it later, but was soon immersed in my day, meeting with family members and conducting new patient intakes. I was prepared to work right through lunch when there was a knock on my door.

"Come in."

Shirley Delabrey breezed into the room with a confidence that I'd not seen before. She stood more upright and more relaxed. Even her corrugator and glabellar muscles had relaxed, giving her eyes and mouth a warm and receptive expression. Mason shadowed in behind her.

After they sat down, Shirley explained, somewhat proudly, that she was getting divorced and would be getting her own condo, at least for the immediate future. Dilly would live with her, and Mason was also welcome to stay. Mason, though, seemed non-committal. Then, as an afterthought she added, "Oh, Mason's been released, too!"

"Really? I didn't know that. I haven't seen the discharge

plan. Can I help?"

"They've got me scheduled for some groups," shrugged Mason.

"Shirley, do you mind if I have a moment with Mason alone?"

Shirley thanked me, gave me her usual hug and kiss, then stepped outside.

"Mason, I've been wanting to talk to you about your father."

"Why?" he said with a grimace, his jaw clenching.

"When you're wounded by someone, it's normal to reject their qualities and everything about them."

"Yeah. I don't want to be anything like him. He's hurt a lot of people."

"I know, but we need to understand that everyone is mixed."

"Mixed?"

"What I mean is… just remember that no one is either all bad or all good. If you look close enough, we're all mixed. One day you might see how some of your father's qualities are useful. So you can bring them inside."

"Okay," he said in a questioning tone. "You mean like his strengths?"

"Yeah, like strengths. Remember, he's evolving too. We all are. Okay?"

"Okay, thanks, Dr. Banks. I'll try to remember that."

To better shift the context of our conversation to something more personal, I got out of my chair and sat next to Mason.

"I talked with my wife, Beth, and there's the chance you could stay with us. I don't know what you're planning at this stage, but there's a good art program at the college not far from the house. It's an option."

"I'm not sure yet. But thanks for asking. I'll think about it. Anyhow, I'll stay in touch." He stood up.

"Mason, last night. Did you… you know, travel… and visit me?"

"Wow. I didn't think you'd know."

We hugged, and as he disappeared around the corner of the hall, I had a feeling I wouldn't be seeing him again.

Chapter 30

For the next couple of days, I crisscrossed the neighborhood asking about Traveler Jacki, but no one had seen her. As far as I could tell, she had vanished. I remembered that she had mentioned a train station, and I knew it began with the letter A, but I couldn't pin it down. Suddenly, *Albina* popped into my head. I was almost positive that was the name of the train yard she was looking for when I first met her. The Albina Yard.

It was dusk by the time I arrived at the yard. This gray and drab industrial hub of the city was new to me. I was expecting a few tracks and a few trains, but not an entire city of trains. I parked outside the gate, which was patrolled by a heavyset man in a uniform. Was he one of those *bulls* Traveler Jacki warned me about?

Maybe he was, because he gruffly warned me that no one was permitted inside the yard. I don't quite know why, but I had a strong feeling about the man, who was around my age. I told him I was very worried about my son, who I thought was going to hop a train and head South, and could he help me? The man's demeanor softened.

"I got a boy." I could feel the ache in him, the loss. "Only trains going south are down at that end." He pointed. "Go around on the perimeter and don't cross any tracks. It's dangerous."

The air was frigid, and a light dusting of snow started to fall. I stopped to observe the scene, which held a certain beauty. Funny, but I'd started to pause and notice these kinds of moments more frequently. That's when I heard a deep hum, combined with a rumble beneath my feet. A train started to creep along, and when I ran closer, I saw the freight cars, what must have been a hundred or more, slowly bounding side to side as if dancing a two-step.

Two figures bolted out from under an adjacent train, no more than fifty feet away. I could clearly make out Traveler Jacki, with the white feather beside her head. But she was blocking my view of her companion.

"Hey, hey! Traveler Jacki!" I shouted at the top of my lungs while running alongside the train. It didn't look like the wheels were spinning very fast, but I could barely keep up. The person in front of Jacki grabbed onto a handle and easily jumped inside a boxcar. Meanwhile, Traveler Jacki was running as fast as she could, with poor Bear bouncing up and down, clinging to her shoulders for dear life.

Just as Jacki's acquaintance grabbed her outstretched hands and pulled her to safety, she glanced back. "Safe travels, Traveler Ben!" she yelled, vanishing into the boxcar. A moment later, her travel companion popped his head out, his long, jet-black hair flying in the wind. He waved and grinned.

"Mason!" I yelled as loudly as I could. But my legs and lungs were spent. I bent over, hands on knees, exhaling miniature contrails into the air. When I finally stood up, the three Travelers were far off in the distance, still waving at me, until their boxcar disappeared from view.

When I got back to the train yard gate, I thanked the *bull*.

"Ya' see him?"

I could only nod, choked up, my lips shaking. I tried to say "thank you," and although nothing came out, the words were in my eyes and my face. As I looked at this man, I suddenly saw myself, all my frailties and faults, all my longings and losses, all my dreams and desires, reflected in his eyes, his soul.

That's when I knew that we were all seekers, all stardust Travelers on this small blue planet, trying to do our best to make sense of this deliciously implausible existence. And if we couldn't solve anything, the least we could do was to help other Travelers who we met on this fleeting journey.

I sat in my car for a while, sitting in the cold, until darkness descended. I was happy that Mason had decided to travel. There were so few opportunities nowadays for true rites of passage for young men, that this felt right.

The snowflakes continued falling, each a little crystalline miracle. When the entire rail yard was covered in white, I knew it was time to go home. Maybe I'd even try to solve the Rubik's Cube that had befuddled me for so long. Better yet, I'd stop by the nursery and surprise Beth with a Christmas tree.

But first, I got out of the car and did something I hadn't done since high school. I lay down in the snow and made the sweeping shape of angel wings with my arms and legs. Looking up at the snow laden expanse, I thought I heard Traveler Jacki's voice.

Breathe out the noise in your head, Traveler Ben. Breathe in the space. Let yourself grow big, bigger than the sky. Let the little body go. Let it fill with love and light.

I could feel myself growing bigger, bigger than the sky, with no beginning and no ending. A massive vibration roared through my spine, head and body, and the snowflakes assumed the shape of pearly strands. Again, I found myself in a living-breathing multi-dimensional library of light. The sparkling illumination reminded me of the last Christmas that Beth, Melissa and I had shared together. Last year, however, Beth and I had skipped the holidays altogether. That's when a flickering image of Melissa appeared in the distance. She stood next to a beautifully bedecked Christmas tree adorned in colorful ornaments and glimmering lights.

After a moment's focus, I traveled right next to her. We didn't say anything, and though no words were exchanged, I could sense her saying, "Everything will be all right, Dad." Just then, a small Goldfinch alighted on her shoulder. She smiled at the bird and then at me, as if to affirm, "Yes, this was my message to you." I promised myself right then not to take the little things for granted.

I could hardly swallow, overwhelmed with joy. I was surprised when she reached out, and I swear I felt her hand gently caress my face. The entire dimension glowed and glistened with love. It was sublime, and I felt my own heart soften and grow tender. I could have stayed there forever, but it occurred to me that life wasn't meant to be lived in a library, but out in the world, "one breath at a time," as Traveler Jacki had once told me.

The sound of rumbling trains, screeching metal wheels and a lyrical flute echoed throughout the heavens. I couldn't tell if the sound was outside of me or inside, until, unexpectedly, I felt my body shivering on the snowy ground. I sat up just in time to hear a train's distant, lonely rumble.

Just then, as I wished for one final chance to bid farewell to my fellow Travelers Jacki, Mason and Bear, a cloudburst of butterflies formed cursive letters that filled the snowy sky.

Safe Travels, it said.

And yes, I may have squinted.

About the Author

Donald Altman is a psychotherapist, award-winning author, and former Buddhist monk who writes the *Practical Mindfulness Blog* for *Psychology Today*. Profiled in *The Living Spiritual Teachers Project* and featured in *The Mindfulness Movie*, he has written over 15 books that teach how to incorporate mindfulness and greater awareness into daily life. Award-winning books include: *The Mindfulness Toolbox* —winner of two Gold IBPA Benjamin Franklin Awards as best book in the "Psychology" and "Body-Mind-Spirit" categories, *Clearing Emotional Clutter*—selected "One of the Best Spiritual Books of 2016" and *The Mindfulness Code*—chosen "One of the Best Spiritual Books of 2010."

Donald served as vice-president of the international organization, *The Center for Mindful Eating*. He spent years as an adjunct professor in Portland State University's Interpersonal Neurology Certificate Program and at Lewis and Clark Graduate School of Education and Counseling.

He is committed to spreading seeds of kindness and reflective living in his work as an international keynote speaker, consultant, and workshop leader. He lives in Portland, Oregon, enjoying the beauty and awe of nature with his beloved wife, family and friends.

For more info: mindfulpractices.com

Join Donald's Reflect community at: Facebook.com/MndfulPractices

Note from Donald Altman:

Thank you for purchasing *Travelers*. I hope this book was as enjoyable and meaningful for you to read as it was for me to write. If you have a few moments, please feel free to add your review of the book to your favorite online site for feedback.

Also, if you would like to connect with my future work and books, please visit my website and sign up for my newsletter at: http://www.mindfulpractices.com.

Sincerely, Traveler Donald

ROUNDFIRE
BOOKS

FICTION

Put simply, we publish great stories. Whether it's literary or popular, a gentle tale or a pulsating thriller, the connecting theme in all Roundfire fiction titles is that once you pick them up you won't want to put them down.

If you have enjoyed this book, why not tell other readers by posting a review on your preferred book site.

Recent bestsellers from Roundfire are:

The Bookseller's Sonnets
Andi Rosenthal

The Bookseller's Sonnets intertwines three love stories with a tale of religious identity and mystery spanning five hundred years and three countries.

Paperback: 978-1-84694-342-3 ebook: 978-184694-626-4

Birds of the Nile
An Egyptian Adventure
N.E. David

Ex-diplomat Michael Blake wanted a quiet birding trip up the Nile – he wasn't expecting a revolution.

Paperback: 978-1-78279-158-4 ebook: 978-1-78279-157-7

The Cause
Roderick Vincent

The second American Revolution will be a fire lit from an internal spark.

Paperback: 978-1-78279-763-0 ebook: 978-1-78279-762-3

Blood Profit$
The Lithium Conspiracy
J. Victor Tomaszek, James N. Patrick, Sr.
The blood of the many for the profits of the few… *Blood Profit$* will take you into the cigar-smoke-filled room where American policy and laws are really made.
Paperback: 978-1-78279-483-7 ebook: 978-1-78279-277-2

The Burden
A Family Saga
N.E. David
Frank will do anything to keep his mother and father apart. But he's carrying baggage – and it might just weigh him down …
Paperback: 978-1-78279-936-8 ebook: 978-1-78279-937-5

Don't Drink and Fly
The Story of Bernice O'Hanlon: Part One
Cathie Devitt
Bernice is a witch living in Glasgow. She loses her way in her life and wanders off the beaten track looking for the garden of enlightenment.
Paperback: 978-1-78279-016-7 ebook: 978-1-78279-015-0

Gag
Melissa Unger
One rainy afternoon in a Brooklyn diner, Peter Howland punctures an egg with his fork. Repulsed, Peter pushes the plate away and never eats again.
Paperback: 978-1-78279-564-3 ebook: 978-1-78279-563-6

The Master Yeshua
The Undiscovered Gospel of Joseph
Joyce Luck
Jesus is not who you think he is. The year is 75 CE. Joseph ben Jude
is frail and ailing, but he has a prophecy to fulfil ...
Paperback: 978-1-78279-974-0 ebook: 978-1-78279-975-7

On the Far Side, There's a Boy
Paula Coston
Martine Haslett, a thirty-something 1980s woman, plays hard on
the fringes of the London drag club scene until one night which
prompts her to sign up to a charity. She writes to a young Sri
Lankan boy, with consequences far and long.
Paperback: 978-1-78279-574-2 ebook: 978-1-78279-573-5

Tuareg
Alberto Vazquez-Figueroa
With over 5 million copies sold worldwide, *Tuareg* is a classic
adventure story from best-selling author Alberto Vazquez-
Figueroa, about honour, revenge and a clash of cultures.
Paperback: 978-1-84694-192-4

Readers of ebooks can buy or view any of these bestsellers by
clicking on the live link in the title. Most titles are published in
paperback and as an ebook. Paperbacks are available in traditional
bookshops. Both print and ebook formats are available online.

Find more titles and sign up to our readers' newsletter at
http://www.johnhuntpublishing.com/fiction

Follow us on Facebook at https://www.facebook.com/JHPfiction
and Twitter at https://twitter.com/JHPFiction